CHANGE of HEART

Never Say Never...

NIKKI R MILLER

Change of Heart

This book is a work of fiction. Names, characters, places and incidents are products of the author's imagination or are used fictitiously. Any resemblance to actual events, locales, persons—living or dead, is entirely coincidental.

Ordering Information:
Books may be purchased by contacting the publisher, NRM Faith Based Films, LLC, at P.O. Box 5004, Alpharetta, GA 30023 or by email at nrmiller11@gmail.com.

Cover design by: Enigma Graphics
Formatting by: MADE Write

ISBN: 978-0-9977592-0-4 (Paperback)
ISBN: 978-0-9977592-1-1 (E-book)
Library of Congress Control Number: 2016910569
Printed in the United States of America

Introduction

Have you ever been hurt down to the core of your heart? Of course you have. Who hasn't at some point in their life? Whether it was a huge hurt or a small hurt, we all have. Here lies the question of importance though: Have you forgiven your accuser, your abuser, your mom, dad, sibling, aunt, uncle? What about yourself? There's only one true way to be free of your hurt... and that's with God's help.

Carrying around anger and bitterness in your heart against someone, eats away at your spirit until it affects your health, your sanity and those close to you. Now, the devil's got you right where he wants you. This is how he controls you and links himself to you. You've become his puppet where he has you seeking revenge for false gratification, or he'll cleverly set up traps for you to slip into causing the same hurt to someone else. Now you're repeating the cycle which could bring about a generational curse upon you or your family. Whether you were hurt today, yesterday, a month or so ago or years ago, do yourself a favor. You heard me say YOURSELF... not your accuser, abuser or the one who caused your pain and suffering... even if it was you who caused your own hurt.

Do yourself a favor and forgive yourself or them. You may not ever forget what was done, but that's okay. God didn't say or require us to forget; He said forgive. And then He just didn't leave us with the requirement to forgive. He said, "Beloved, never avenge yourselves, but leave the way open for [God's] wrath; for it is written, Vengeance is

Mine, I will repay (requite), says the Lord." Romans 12:19 AMP.

As you read, you will see how forgiveness does not only bring restoration to you and that specific situation, but also to your entire family's other issues or problems when you surrender that hurt completely to God. You never know... God may use your situation to help someone else OR go on that same forgiving journey together with someone who's struggling also. In this book, you will read about a man named Calvin Hardy Jr. and what he had to endure before overcoming his unforgiveness problem.

Chapter 1

*I*t was a cool, but calm peaceful night in the month of September of 1985 in Southfield, Michigan. On the corner of Feldman Avenue, a dark blue 1983 Ford LTD Sedan pulled into the driveway of a nice one-story tan brick home alongside a white 1979 old looking Ford F-150. Rose Hardy, an average looking attractive medium skin toned thirty-eight-year-old African-American woman wearing a white nurse's uniform with Southfield General Hospital stitched on it, slowly got out of the car on the driver side. Her hair was pulled back into a bun. In her left hand was her purse and in the right was a red and white striped box with KFC printed on the side.

As she plodded toward the front door, she took a glimpse through a window and saw flickering lights coming from a television inside. A quick smile came upon her weary face as she discerned that it was her thirteen-year-old son watching T.V. and most likely, football. His name, Calvin

Hardy Jr., a handsome, athletically built African-American boy who adored his mom and hoped to someday see her face in the stands at a pro football game of his. He was sitting on the sofa still in his gym shorts and practice jersey which said McArthur Middle School Football. The living room area was filled with a stench of musk in the air. He heard her at the door and opened it with haste to let her in as he anticipated her coming in carrying something to eat. A savory aroma of fried chicken clashed with the smell of musk, but it went unnoticed. Calvin Jr. then hurried back to the sofa as if he was going to miss something important in the football game he was watching.

There were only two lights glaring in the home, the one coming from the T.V. and the one coming from Rose's bedroom which was a few steps away from the living room. The home was decorated conservatively with limited furniture; however, pleasant. And a few family pictures were on the wall and on end tables in the living room.

"Thanks, Junior," Rose said with a sigh, then smiled when she glanced at the T.V. as she took the box into the kitchen knowing her hunch was right about her son.

A man angrily yelled, "Where you been, Rose?" from a bedroom. He was a somewhat tall and handsome forty-year-old African-American man with a mustache and goatee named Calvin Hardy Sr. who was a construction worker and

Calvin Jr.'s dad, the man Calvin, Jr. resembled and looked up to.

Calvin Sr. stood in front of his and Rose's bedroom door wearing a white wife beater and some old rugged jeans as he waited for Rose's response.

She yelled from the kitchen, "I stopped to get us something to eat." Then, she walked back into the living room. She said to her son, "Junior, go get you some chicken."

"Okay, yes ma'am," Calvin Jr. answered. He proceeded to prance toward the kitchen until Rose stopped him dead in his tracks.

"Wash those hands young man."

"Yes, ma'am," Calvin Jr. answered as he headed to the bathroom.

Rose proceeded to her bedroom, passing in front of Calvin Sr. at the doorway without a word to him.

"Rose, I know it didn't take this long for you to get home from work."

"Calvin, I got off at seven, then stopped to get dinner for us. What is the big deal?" Rose asked. She pulled open a drawer on her dresser and began rummaging through her clothes to find something more comfortable to put on.

Calvin Sr. grasped Rose's arm tightly.

"Ou—!"

"Don't lie to me, Rose!" her husband said abruptly.

3

At the sound of her outcry, Calvin Jr. immediately dropped the chicken leg he was feasting on, onto the floor while in the kitchen and rushed to his parents' bedroom door to see what was going on. Rose had a look of complete confusion on her face because his behavior had been off lately. He was normally a mild-tempered, church-going man.

Rose snatched away from her husband and yelled, "I'm not!"

"Momma, you alright?" Calvin Jr. asked.

"Junior, this don't concern you! Go eat!" his dad said with attempted calmness. However, it went in one ear and out the other.

Calvin Jr. stood right where he was. "Momma?"

Rose responded calmly with, "Just do what he said, baby. I'm fine."

Calvin Jr. walked slowly to his bedroom, slamming the door. Then into the closet he went. He plopped down on his butt and covered his ears with his hands as if he'd been through this before. The bickering continued between Rose and Calvin Sr.

"I think you seeing another man!" said Calvin Sr.

"I'm not seeing anybody! I love you too much to do that! You need to get your facts straight!"

Calvin Sr. stuck his right index finger in Rose's face and said, "Well if I find out you lying to me, you gone be sorry!" He backed away from her. "I'll be back! I need to cool off."

Rose said quickly, "Yeah, you do."

Her husband stormed out of their bedroom and out of the front door. Calvin Jr. peeked his head out of the closet to make sure the coast was clear.

Then, he rushed to his mom. He asked, "Momma, you sure you alright?"

"Yeah, I'm fine, Junior," she responded. "Something is off about that man. I don't know what it is."

"I know you're telling the truth, Momma," he said.

"I know you do. Junior, hand me my purse, please?" Rose asked as she sat at the foot of her bed. Calvin Jr. grabbed the same black purse Rose had when she came into the house and handed it over to his mom with a look of curiosity. "Thank you, baby." Rose unzipped the top of her purse, reached inside and pulled out a black jewelry box with Seiko engraved on the top of it. She opened the jewelry box as if it was an oyster revealing, not a pearl, but a stunning Seiko men's stainless steel yellow gold plated quartz watch.

"Is that mine, Momma?" Calvin Jr. asked excitedly.

Rose giggled under her breath and said, "No, it's your dad's. I was out getting this for his birthday. Remember his birthday is on Sunday."

"Yeah, I forgot," her son said, as if he could care less. Then asked, "Why didn't you just tell him?"

"He didn't give me a chance to, Junior. And I wanted to surprise him with it on Sunday," she explained.

Calvin Jr. blurted, "He don't deserve it!" Then covered his mouth as if he was ashamed at what he had said.

"Yeah, I know. He'll see where I was, on Sunday after he get his gift," she said. "God always bless us with things we don't deserve. That is what you call mercy, Junior… Something we get over and over again, even when we do wrong," Rose shared with her son, instilling that truth in him.

Chapter 2

*I*t was Sunday morning around 10:45 am, the sun was shining bright and the temperature was somewhat cool, yet pleasant. Cars were still parking and people were scurrying to the church doors to get inside for service at Greater Love Baptist Church, a small white church that had been there for years nestled in a quiet Southfield community.

Calvin Sr., Rose and Calvin Jr. were among those scurrying in to make sure they wouldn't be a distraction to the congregation. They were dressed in their Sunday best: Calvin Sr. with a black polyester suit, white dress shirt, and a matching paisley tie and handkerchief that was white, purple and black. Every strand of hair was laying down on his head to show he had a fresh haircut and not one hair was sticking out of his mustache or goatee. Rose's attire consisted of a burgundy fall hat trimmed in rosette and loops with a rhinestone brooch, a beautiful burgundy matching skirt and jacket with a silk white blouse. Her hair, full of curls, peeked out from under her hat. Calvin Jr. was also sporting his best, just like his dad: a black polyester suit with a mustard color shirt, along with a black and mustard tie. Although a rugged and tough guy, he enjoyed dressing up like his dad.

Calvin Sr. opened the door to allow his family to go in. Then his eyes fixated upon a thirty-six-year-old pretty and stylish African-American church member by the name of Sister Arlene West, who was headed toward the church doors as well. She was adorned with an elegant royal blue wide brim hat that somewhat hid her face and a pretty floral print fitting dress with a hint of royal blue in it.

Calvin said quickly, "Rose, you and Junior can go on in."

"We can wait for you," said Rose.

"No, I'll be in, in a minute," he told her.

She was puzzled by his response, but continued into the church, along with Calvin Jr. "Alright, then," Rose said.

Calvin Sr. closed the door behind them and then waited patiently to have the honor of opening the door again for the next person.

"Morning, Sister Arlene," Calvin Sr. said proudly with a faint smile.

"Good morning, Deacon Hardy," she said politely.

"You looking mighty fine this morning."

"Why, thank you," she responded, as if she already knew that, but took the compliment anyway. As she proceeded to reach for the door, Calvin Sr. beat her to it.

"Oh, let me get that for you," he said, showing off his gentleman attributes.

Sister Arlene strutted in and took a seat in the middle section of the congregation on the left side. Calvin Sr. strolled in and took his seat with the other deacons up at the front of the church on the left side of the pulpit. Rose was seated with the deaconess up at the front of the church on the right side of the pulpit. Calvin Jr. was also on the right side, but in the main section along with the rest of the congregation. He was sitting with his best friend, Tony Brown better known as T.B., a quiet average, but nice looking thirteen-year-old African-American boy who was a little shorter than Calvin Jr.

As the choir marched in to "We're Marching Up to Zion", a stout fiftyish year old African-American man by the name of Deacon Lloyd Barnes, entered into the sanctuary from a door by the choir stand and came over to Calvin Sr.

"Deacon Hardy, can you do devotion with Deacon Mays this morning?" Deacon Barnes asked.

Calvin Sr. said, "Sure. You already told Deacon Mays?"

"Yeah, he knows," Deacon Barnes responded and then took his seat in the deacon section.

The choir had completed their processional and was now seated in the choir stand in their perspective places. Calvin Sr. and Deacon Everett Mays, a somewhat tall and slim forty-five-year-old African-American deacon, strolled over to a small dark wooden table with two chairs facing the congregation and centered below the pulpit. A small black book was sitting on the table by it's lonesome. They both pulled the table out a little so they could stand in front of the chairs. With excitement, Calvin Sr. began speaking to the congregation.

"God is good all the time, and all the time God is good. Amen?"

"Amen," the congregation said faintly.

He shouted, "I said, Amen?"

"Amen!" the congregation shouted back.

Calvin Sr. then inched the small black book over to him and began flipping the pages to find the hymn he wanted to sing. As the congregation waited in anticipation for him, he concealed his fumbling by conversing with the congregation. Some in the congregation giggled and snickered at him because they were well aware of what he was doing.

"Well, I'm blessed because today God has allowed me to see another birthday! I won't tell you how old I am because I don't want you all calling me old. And don't go asking my wife either." He chuckled a little as he had finally found the hymn. "Well, everyone join in with me and sing Hymn #413. *A charge to keep I have, A God to glorify. A never dying soul to save and fit it for the sky."*

The congregation followed suit and delivered what he asked.

Not long after, Deacon Mays casually got down on one knee and bellowed out a prayer that could be heard miles away. Some eyes were gazed upon him with awe instead of bowing their heads, especially children. He entertained the children for a good five minutes and then turned the service over to Reverend Tolbert. The service finally made its way to the benediction as church goers poured out of the doors, ready to sit at someone's table to partake of some long-awaited vittles, except for a few church mothers who remained behind. They could care less about the growl going on in one's stomach. They wanted to gab. Calvin Sr. and Rose became recipients of that gabbing, despite their reluctance.

"Alright mothers, we gotta go. My wife has cooked me a surprise birthday meal and I'm ready to eat it," he told them while giving Rose a hint with eye contact.

Rose aided in his escape by saying, "Well mothers, we'll see ya next Sunday. Have a blessed week." Then she and her husband politely hightailed out of there to their car. However, they were delayed in their escape when they saw

Calvin Jr. afar off hanging out with his buddy, T.B., as if he drove to church and had all the time in the world.

Rose yelled, "Junior, come on! We're ready!" Then yelled, "Bye T.B."

Calvin Jr. and Tony gave each other dap. "I'll get up wit'cha later, T.B., after I eat," Calvin Jr. said.

Tony answered, "Alright."

Then Calvin Jr. proceeded with haste to the car so he would be allowed to later hang out with Tony.

Chapter 3

*B*ack at home, Rose was ecstatic to reveal what all she had cooked for her husband's birthday dinner. She wasted no time in transitioning into something more comfortable along with her apron, and began warming up the feast. You would have thought it was Thanksgiving in their home. The aroma in the air was heavenly with the smell of a honey baked ham, collard greens, potato salad and corn bread. And there was a hint of a sweet aroma of chocolate in the air saying, "don't forget about me sitting over here." A chocolate cake sat by itself on the counter waiting to be devoured also. Rose gathered portions of each dish, except dessert, and carefully placed them on a plate or in a bowl to dress the table. The table was already covered with a white tablecloth, dinner plates, silverware and glasses along with a pitcher of tea.

Rose yelled, "Calvin, I cooked you a *nice* birthday dinner. So hurry and wash up… both of you." She smiled as she took a moment to inspect her presentation before leaving the kitchen.

Calvin Jr. and his dad entered the kitchen with wide eyes as they stared at the spread on the table. Then, they quickly took a seat. To curtail his watering mouth, Calvin Sr. grabbed the pitcher of tea and poured himself some in a glass that was sitting in front of him.

Then he said, "We have people coming over, Junior?"

"I don't think so. Momma just wanted to cook you a nice meal since it's your birthday," Calvin Jr. answered.

Rose slipped back into the kitchen carrying the Seiko jewelry box behind her back and placed it on the counter, out of her husband's view, then took her rightful place at the table.

"Alright, I'm gonna say grace. I've been trying to hold off from digging in. Lord, thank you for this food we're about to receive and for allowing me to spend another birthday with my family. Amen," he prayed.

Calvin Jr. began loading up his plate the second he heard 'Amen' come out of his dad's mouth. His parents did the same not long after him. Then each of them began devouring their favorites on their plates first.

"Those mothers were trying to get you to say your age, huh?" Rose asked while somewhat chuckling.

Her husband answered, "Yeah, they were trying." before taking a bite of his golden buttery corn bread. Then he chuckled a little.

"I don't know why you were being so secretive about it. You don't look *that* old," Rose told him as she smiled.

"Yes he does, Momma," Calvin Jr. insisted, as he interrupted his mom and dad's conversation.

Rose couldn't help but laugh at him.

His dad responded, "I'm not old, Junior. You don't see no grey on this face or on my head."

Rose snuck away from the table while her husband and son were conversing, and grabbed the jewelry box.

"That's because you dye it, Daddy."

His dad sat there speechless, wondering how his son knew that. Rose was tickled. She came back to the table and placed the jewelry box in front of her husband, then took her seat and began eating again.

"What's this, Rose?" Calvin Sr. asked, attempting to be surprised. He knew he would get something in addition to dinner for his birthday, but had been wondering what it would be.

Rose replied, "Open it and see."

"Open it, Daddy," Calvin Jr. said impatiently.

15

His dad finally pried open the jewelry box revealing the watch. His eyes grew wide as a slow grin came upon his face.

"Happy Birthday!" Rose told her husband.

With less excitement, Calvin Jr. said, "Happy Birthday, Daddy," as he remembered how he treated his mom when she returned home from buying that watch.

"So when did you have time to get this?" his dad asked his mom.

Rose answered, "On Friday, after work... the same night I brought the chicken home."

Calvin Jr. couldn't wait to hear what his dad had to say after his mom's response. He put his right elbow on the table, then relaxed his hand up under his chin with his eyes glued on his dad.

"You should've told me, Rose!" A feeling of guilt and shame came upon his dad.

Calvin Jr. sternly said, "You didn't give her a chance to, Daddy!" He quickly went into protection mode as he envisioned hearing his mom's outburst on Friday night.

Rose sensed the anger building up in her son. And said, "Junior, it's alright. Let's just enjoy dinner," to calm him down.

"Rose, I'm sorry 'bout that. You know I just act before thinking sometimes," her husband explained in hopes of obtaining understanding and sympathy from his wife and son.

Rose said, "It's fine," attempting to forget about what happened on that evening. "So, you like it?"

"Yeah... it's nice. Thank you," he said while lifting the watch out of the box to admire it closely. "And you too, Junior," he told his son, which seemed to lift the anger that was building up in Calvin Jr.

With a slight smile on his face, he responded, "You're welcome Daddy, even though it wasn't my money that bought it. So, are you gone let me borrow it sometimes?" he asked, hoping he was apologetic enough to say yes.

"Maybe, when you get a little older," he answered.

Of course, it wasn't the answer Calvin Jr. was expecting. He really did believe his dad was going to say yes. "How much older? I think I'm old enough now, Daddy."

His dad replied, "Old enough where you can replace it, if you break it," as he wore a slight smirk on his face.

"Yeah, that'll work. I can wait," he told his dad without any objection.

His parents chuckled at his response. His dad placed his watch back in the jewelry box and focused his attention on the homemade chocolate cake sitting on the counter waiting to be devoured by anyone that pleased. He quickly shoved his plate to the side and cleared off any leftovers from his mouth with a napkin.

"Is that my chocolate cake over there?" Knowing that it was, Calvin's dad still asked with a large grin on his face.

With a smile, his mom answered, "Maybe. What do you think? And I'm guessing you want some of it since you pushed your plate to the side." She stood up to fetch a knife and two plates. She cut a huge hunk for her husband and a sizable slice for her son, then served both of them as if she were their waitress. She still had not gotten through all of the food on her plate yet.

Calvin's dad plunged into his slice after taking a swipe of chocolate with his finger and licking it off until there was no more. Calvin Jr. was still going at the ham and collard greens on his plate ensuring to eat every morsel on it.

"You know who else at church is crazy about chocolate cake?" his dad asked his mom.

"Who? Reverend Tolbert?"

"No, Deacon Barnes. I told him whenever you make another one, I would bring him some. Rose, you mind cutting him a piece? And I'll take it to him. I'm sure he'll love that."

Calvin Jr. said, "That man don't need any cake, Daddy...with his potbelly self."

His mom giggled slightly. She knew her son was telling the truth. She said, "That's true, Junior." Then said to her husband, "He can stand to miss a few desserts, Calvin. And a few meals, if you ask me." She and her son broke out into full laughter.

Calvin Jr.'s dad said, "Hey..." admonishing his wife and son, until he began contemplating what his wife said. Then joined in the circle of laughter. "Yeah, I know," he admitted.

After settling down from laughing, Calvin Jr. asked, "Daddy, is it okay if I ride my bike to T.B.'s house?"

His dad replied, "Yeah, that's fine, Junior," as he scraped the last bit of chocolate icing off of his plate with his fork while simmering down from laughing at Deacon Barnes. Rose had already put an end to her giggling so she could try and finish eating what was left on her plate.

"Just be back before it gets dark," said Rose.

"Yes ma'am. Momma, I'll eat my cake later." Eager to hang out with T.B., Calvin Jr. quickly carried his empty dinner plate to the sink and placed his cake on the counter. Then, he dashed out of the kitchen, heading to the bathroom to wash his hands, before he grabbed his bike. Rose had taken in all she could eat, leaving a few scraps on her plate. So she went on ahead and got up from the table to cut a sizable slice of chocolate cake for Deacon Barnes, and wrapped it up in a piece of aluminum foil. She then placed it in front of her husband.

"Rose, I'll be back. I'm gonna go ahead and take Deacon Barnes his cake while it's still early."

"Alright. Tell him I said enjoy… and put in a little exercise to go with it." Rose chuckled.

Her husband called out, "Rose!" with a slight smile on his face. He knew what she said was funny, but wouldn't admit it.

"I'm just kidding," Rose told him with a slight grin on her face still.

He shook his head in disbelief at what his wife had just said, but was still tickled on the inside which was evidenced by him smiling. He arose from the table, grabbed Deacon Barnes' cake and departed the kitchen, leaving the house.

Rose stood between the kitchen table and sink with her hands on her hips surveying what was on the table, the dishes in the sink and the pots and pans on the stove. And thought to herself, "How did I let that happen? Now who's going to help me clean up this mess?" After realizing she was the only one left in the house to do it, she began the grueling task.

Chapter 4

*T*he afternoon was pleasant outside, although a little cool; the sun was still peeking through to shine its warmth. Calvin Jr. rolled up to T.B.'s home on his blue and black BMX bike ready to possibly partake in some innocent mischief, although they weren't troublesome boys; just boys that liked to have a little fun every now and then. They would sometimes ride their bikes to a small pond near their homes to engage in a little fishing; however, most of the time would only catch just that... time instead of fish. Or they would ride their bikes around the neighborhood scouting out interesting people to talk about, such as people who carried a lot of extra weight on their bodies. Most of the time however, they would just trade off going to each other's homes to play games. Neither one of them really had any other friends. It was just the two of them always.

T.B. lived just a couple of blocks away from Calvin Jr. in a charming white brick home; however, not as nice or big as his. Sometimes he would make comparisons out loud whenever he was mad at T.B. for something, comparing everything he could think of which included their bodies. In the end, they always found themselves hanging out together as if they were blood brothers. For one, Calvin Jr. didn't have any siblings. T.B. had two sisters, but they are much older. So, you can say he might as well be an only child.

Once at T.B.'s home, he pulled in the driveway, kicked out the kickstand on his bike and dismounted it. He quickly approached the front door of T.B.'s home, knocking on it. Already expecting Calvin Jr., T.B. opened the door without inquiring or hesitating. He was dressed in play clothes, jeans and a regular T-shirt, the same as Calvin Jr. was wearing.

"What's up, C.J.?"

"Can you come out now?" Calvin Jr. asked.

"Yeah, I can. You wanna play football here?"

"Play football where, T.B.? As soon as you throw the football to me, I'll have a touchdown by *walking* to the end zone. There's no room," said Calvin Jr. "We can go to my house and play. And then eat some of the chocolate cake my momma made." A slight smirk came upon his face as mentioned the chocolate cake. He knew T.B. wouldn't turn down eating chocolate cake.

"Alright. Let me get my bike," answered T.B. Then, he stepped outside of his home and closed the front door behind him. He hurried to the side and grabbed his dark green BMX bike. It wasn't as decked out as Calvin Jr.'s, of course, but he still rolled it with care to his driveway where Calvin Jr.'s bike was. They both mounted their bikes and took off to Calvin Jr.'s home. In the midst of riding, they decided to take somewhat of a different route, just for fun and to make the ride a little longer. It was a nice day and there was still plenty of time before it would get dark. So they took advantage of that. All they did was ride another two blocks past T.B.'s house, making a loop so that now instead of Calvin Jr.'s home being two blocks away, it was now four blocks away. The boys decided to stop at the second block past T.B.'s house to take a little break from riding and scope out the neighborhood for anybody they could talk about.

While exploring, Calvin Jr. spotted what looked like to be his dad's pick-up truck. It had construction materials in the back of it like he normally had, but he was still uncertain if it really was his dad's truck. The truck was parked in a driveway not far from the street corner where Calvin Jr. and T.B. was parked.

"Hey T.B., that look like my dad's truck," Calvin Jr. said. Moments later, sure enough Calvin Sr. got out of the truck and strolled into a pleasant sky colored blue brick home. "Wait a minute… that is my dad. He just walked into that house." He pondered a moment. "That's not Deacon Barnes house!"

T.B. asked, "You know the people that stay there?" He was curious also.

"No, come on," he summoned T.B. and they cruised over to the home on their bikes. They stopped in front of the home, dismounted, and laid their bikes down on the sidewalk. Sneaking over to a side window, they kneeled down and took a peek inside.

Calvin Jr.'s heart felt like it dropped to the pit of his stomach as he witnessed his dad sitting on a sofa with his arm around a woman. It was none other than Sister Arlene West from their church. She was holding the wrapped up cake that his mom had cut for Deacon Barnes. The boys watched Sister Arlene as she peeled the foil back revealing the chocolate cake and then pinched off a piece to taste it.

T.B. murmured, "Hey, doesn't she go to our church?"

"Yeah… she does," answered Calvin Jr. with anger.

"Shh… you don't want your dad to find out we're here, do you?" T.B. murmured.

Calvin Jr. continued to stare in dismay as Sister Arlene and his dad stood up from the sofa and went into her bedroom, closing the door behind them.

"No," he murmured angrily.

T.B. whispered, "Man, so your dad's cheating?" And then he pondered. "But he's a deacon! He's not allowed to do that," he said as he put two and two together.

"I know, T.B.!" Calvin Jr. stood up and began heading back to his bike. T.B. did the same. They went unnoticed by his dad and Sister Arlene. Calvin Jr. exclaimed, "He lied to my mom! He was supposed to be taking cake over to Deacon Barnes. I hate him!" And then, he mounted his bike, abandoning T.B. without thought.

"C.J., wait!" shouted T.B.; however, his friend was long gone. With a solemn face, T.B. headed back to his house on his bike. He really felt bad for his friend.

Calvin Jr. pulled up to his home and hopped off his bike, slamming it down onto the ground in the driveway then, stormed into the house rushing to his bedroom. He closed his door, leaving a crack and then plopped down on his bed with his eyes full of water.

His mom had finally completed the daunting task of tidying up the kitchen and was unwinding at the kitchen table with an Essence magazine and a cup of Folgers. She heard the front door closed, but wasn't going to interrupt her time of relaxation. She knew it had to only be her son. If it was her husband, she knew he would find her so he could tell her about what Deacon Barnes thought about the cake.

"Junior, is that you?" she called out from the kitchen. There was no answer. She thought maybe he just didn't hear

25

her. She knew it was him, but just wanted to confirm. So she left the comfort of her magazine and coffee to inquire.

The door of Calvin Jr.'s bedroom was somewhat cracked open and not one sound was coming from the inside. Rose lightly tapped on the door and peeked her head inside before opening it. He attempted to erase the tears from his face before his mom could see them.

She looked at his face and said, "Junior? What's wrong?"

"Momma, daddy's cheating on you!" he angrily declared.

"What? Why would you think your dad is cheating on me, Junior?" Rose was curious as to how he came to that conclusion and she didn't believe him.

He answered, "Because I know…me and T.B. just saw him over at one of the lady's house that go to our church."

"Are you sure you're not mistaking him for someone else?" his mom asked, still in disbelief.

"Yes ma'am, I'm sure. We looked in the window."

Rose was speechless and in a state of shock, not sure of what to say or how to react in front of her son. She turned her back to him for a moment in order to take it all in. Then after a few seconds, she faced him again.

"Who was it?" asked Rose calmly, trying to figure it out in her head; however, she had no clue of who it could be.

Calvin Jr. finally mustered up the strength to be the man his mom needed right now.

He ceased being tearful and said, "I think her last name is West."

"Sister Arlene?" she asked him, but was really asking herself. She began to boil with anger inside while attempting to keep calm for her son's sake. But she could no longer hold it in and let it rip. "That lying son of a b—!"

Calvin Jr. cut her off and quickly yelled, "Sorry, Momma!" desiring to aid in calming his mom down. He didn't want her to revert back to cussing. It wasn't in her nature; in the past it was, but not now. Now he felt rotten for telling his mom. "I didn't want to cause any trouble between you and Daddy," he said sincerely.

"No, he's the one who's gone be sorry. You did nothing wrong, Junior, you only told the truth," she told him.

Calvin Jr. sighed with relief, but still felt bad on the inside.

"I just can't believe he took cake that *I* made for him, over to another woman's house! And had the nerve to accuse me of seeing another man?" she stated aloud.

Suddenly, Calvin Sr. entered through the front door. She pronounced, "Speaking of the devil... literally!" as she paraded into the living room to stop her husband dead in his tracks before coming any further into her home.

Calvin Jr. trailed behind her. "What took you so long, Calvin?" asked Rose, but she didn't wait for a response. "I thought you would've been back by now." She stood there with her arms folded. She still wouldn't let him get a word in; he wasn't ready to say anything anyway. She said, "I didn't think it would take this long to take cake over to Deacon Barnes." She was eager to see just what he was going to say, as she continued to stand there with her arms folded.

Calvin Jr. was waiting also.

He finally replied, "No. We just talked for a while after I gave him the cake. He said to tell you thank you."

With sarcasm, Rose said, "Oh, really?"

Her husband didn't pick up on it though. "Yeah Rose, you should've seen him. As soon as I placed it in his hands, he opened it and ate it."

By this time, Rose was completely irritated with him and fuming inside.

"Calvin, just stop with the lies! Where were you really?"

Dishonesty was portrayed all over his face as he continued to hang on to where he was. "I told you! Why all the questions?" her husband asked.

"Don't you dare bold up at me!" advised Rose. "Your son saw you over at Sister Arlene's."

He peeked around at Calvin Jr. standing behind, but not far off from his mom just in case he needed to protect her from his dad. Calvin Jr. returned an angry look back at his dad.

It finally hit Rose in the gut and she succumbed to the fact that her son was actually telling the truth. She still didn't want to believe it; they were a church going family and held positions in the church. She became tearful as the truth sunk in. That anger began to rise up in Calvin Jr. once more.

Rose asked, "How in God's name, can you accuse me of seeing another man when you're the one who's going behind my back seeing another woman?" He had nothing to say, but a dumbfounded look stayed on his face. Rose then said, "And to make matters worse... someone at our church!" There was a moment of silence where you could hear a pin drop. The tears began to fade as she wiped her face and laid in to him. "Deacon Hardy, that's some example you've set for our son. Now, I want you to get your stuff and get out!" she ordered.

Calvin Sr. was still speechless, yet proceeded to do exactly what she asked.

The day started out as a celebration, but ended up being a day of hurt, especially for Calvin Jr. as he felt this was all his fault. After about fifteen minutes had gone by, his dad came out of their bedroom lugging a huge suitcase in his hand, while he and his mom watched from the living room.

Before heading to the door, he stopped in front of his wife and said, "Rose, I'm sorry."

"I don't wanna hear it, Calvin... Go," she told him, although it grieved her on the inside. "And the church will know about this. I can't and will not lie for you."

Calvin Sr. said, "I know. I wouldn't expect you to." Then he took one last look at his son before leaving out of the front door. "I'm sorry, Junior."

But saying sorry didn't move him one bit at the moment. All he could think of was how his dad hurt his mom after all the trouble she went through for his birthday. And then he wondered even more if his dad had been spending time with Sister Arlene when he claimed he couldn't make it to some of his football games. He would tell his son he had a business meeting at church or had something to do at church. The man he looked up to, was not that man anymore. His dad departed out of the front door without looking back. Calvin Jr. went over to his mom and put his arms around her tightly.

"I'm sorry you had to see that, Junior. I'm so sorry..." expressed Rose.

This overwhelming misfortune would stick with Calvin Jr. for years to come although he tried desperately to forget it. Eventually, their church did find out about what Calvin Sr. did when the deacons and a few church mothers began noticing his absence from church. They questioned

Rose about it at which time she had no choice but to tell them what happened. Calvin Sr. never returned back to that church for fear of embarrassment. With the help and encouragement of her church family and a few family members, Rose was able to work through the hurt caused by her husband. Her family all lived down South, including her parents who she would talk to often.

As years went by, Calvin Sr. would stop by the house every so often to see how his son and wife were doing; however, Calvin Jr. would have nothing to do with him. He would stay in his room or go to T.B.'s house. It was obvious that Rose still cared about her husband, as she would always let him in and talk with him for a little while. Although, she never invited him to move back in. They never officially filed for divorce either. She just couldn't bring herself to date anyone else or remarry.

Ever since his dad was kicked out of the house, Calvin always assumed the responsibility of being the man of the house. He lost the love of playing football after his dad left, and really wasn't interested in other sports or activities. He began working part-time at an auto supply store after school. His dad would give Rose money for him, but he wouldn't accept it. He wanted to earn his own money. In between working and helping out his mom at home, he managed to squeeze in some time for a girlfriend and T.B. He dated a girl at his high school who kept his full attention, in addition to his mom. He had known her since his freshman and sophomore year, but began dating her during his junior year. Her name was Natalie. She was a pretty, wholesome girl who Rose adored. Calvin would bring her over to the house for dinner often when they weren't hanging out with T.B. and his girlfriend.

That was only up until he and T.B. began college at Michigan State University. They both forgot they ever had girlfriends when they arrived there. Their girlfriends had gone on to different colleges. Calvin was now about 5'9", handsome with a medium complexion and still somewhat athletically built. He kept his hair cut low with deep seated waves, and wore a little peach fuzz on his chin. T.B. had grown some too; not as much as Calvin though, but still really nice looking. He was about 5'7". They both always dressed to impress the girls, wearing denim jeans or nice slacks with polo type shirts or casual long sleeve shirts. Calvin stayed on campus with T.B., but checked on his mom every chance he got. He majored in Engineering while T.B. majored in Communications. Calvin's goal was to become a project manager for commercial construction projects, although deep inside, his passion had always been to be a professional football player.

They did just about everything together: attended campus parties, a little clubbing, sought out girls, ate, drank... you name it. Calvin and T.B. attended fraternity parties as well, but never became a part of one. They would always say, "I'm not let'n a grown behind man spank on me, especially if he didn't conceive me." Throughout their college years, they came to know a few guys and girls. But there was one particular girl that Calvin couldn't keep his eyes off of during his junior year. She was a 5"3", twenty-year old cute African-American girl with an hour glass body. Her hair was black, kind of straight with a few curls at the end, and came just past her shoulders. Her complexion was medium and her face without blemishes. The clothing she wore was always fashionable and classy, yet modest.

Her name was Elaina Victoria James. She was at Michigan State studying to be a teacher just like her mom, Norma James. Her mom taught English at a high school. Her dad's name was Fred James. He was a truck driver and had also served in the Army about ten years ago before retiring. Elaina had one sister who was eleven years younger. Fred and Norma ran a tight ship in their household. It was always about church and education in their home. Those standards remained with Elaina throughout her college years and beyond. There was one problem though; Calvin had disconnected himself from church ever since he caught his dad cheating, however, still attended when he lived at home because his mom made him. When he began at Michigan State, he stopped going to church altogether... that was until he met Elaina.

She had a rule, and that rule was whoever dated her, had to attend church with her; at least sometimes. Calvin was okay with that. He could handle going to church just "sometimes" as long as he didn't have to become a part of the church; he just wanted Elaina. Elaina somehow knew he wasn't into church; however, didn't mind because she wanted him also and he honored her rule. Her parents seemed to like him as well just because he was a respectable young man and could tell he really cared for their daughter. And Rose was very pleased with her, especially since she and her family were Christians. Calvin made sure he brought her home to meet his mom and get her approval. Calvin and Elaina became inseparable their last two years of college and beyond graduation. They still would hang out sometimes with their friends, but most of their time was spent together.

After Calvin graduated from college in 1993, he began a two year paid project management internship program with a company called Moreland Enterprises located in Detroit Michigan, making $18.50/hour. With the money he made from them, he was able to obtain his own apartment in Detroit. Elaina continued to live at home in Southfield while she worked on acquiring her master's degree in Education from Michigan State; however, still visited Calvin at his apartment often. She would never sleep over at his apartment though, because she didn't believe in doing that... neither did her parents, although Calvin wouldn't have minded. He tried multiple times to get her to stay, but Elaina desired for her and Calvin to be abstinent until marriage. She had always believed since her senior year in college, Calvin would someday become her husband. She was right.

Whether he was really excited to make that commitment or just plain tired of being abstinent, he took the plunge and proposed. It was a couple of weeks after she had graduated with her master's degree when he popped the question. On the day before though, he stopped by her home without her knowing and obtained permission from her dad. Then on Saturday evening, May 25, 1996, he presented her with a ½ carat preset petite solitaire engagement ring at an elegant steakhouse where he had set up a reservation for him and Elaina. After their meal, he told Elaina he had already ordered dessert for them. He called the waiter over to their table and told him they were ready for the dessert. The waiter returned holding up a platter carrying only a small black ring case. He lowered it down in front of Calvin and Elaina. Her eyes stretched wide open as Calvin grabbed the case, then the waiter left the table. Elaina smiled while Calvin opened the case toward her. Tears began streaming down her face before Calvin could get out the words, "Will you marry me?" She quickly responded with "Yes", then allowed Calvin to place the ring on the ring finger. She didn't realize the proposal would come this soon, but was ready for it. After the ring was placed on her finger, she began to slide it off and said, "You need to ask my Dad." Calvin quickly replied, "That's already been taken care of." Elaina smiled as she thought to herself, "I should've known." Calvin is the kind of person who always know exactly what he wants to do and go for it without delay.

They were married exactly four months from that day, on Saturday, September 28, 1996 in front of God, their family and friends. It wasn't a big wedding, and they had everyone there they desired to be there. Their colors were royal blue and gray. Royal blue was a color that both Calvin and Elaina could agree on and liked. T.B. served as Calvin's best man, of course, while Elaina's college friend Alyssa was her maid of honor. Elaina James was now Elaina Hardy. Rose was so overjoyed that her son had gotten married to a Christian girl. She had notified Calvin's dad that he was getting married prior to the wedding; however, unfortunately, he wasn't privileged to attend the wedding. Calvin still wanted nothing to do with him. After several attempts of calling his son well after his marriage with no response, Calvin Sr. finally gave up on trying to reconnect with him.

As years passed, Calvin's heart continued to hardened toward his dad every time he thought about what he did. Elaina would always try to convince him to call him, just as his mom did; however, Calvin rejected the suggestion.

Elaina was hoping he would change his mind after having children of his own, but it didn't. For the most part, their marriage was harmonious; although he still wasn't into church like Elaina desired for him to be, but just figured he would come around sooner or later. She was just happy that he was going. But in November of 2014, a certain turn of events caused him to go into overdrive with his bitterness.

Chapter 5

"*C*an I get an Amen?" Pastor Ronald Gillesby asked the congregation on this beautiful Sunday morning in November of 2014, at High Faith International Church. It was a rather large church in Southfield, but had a close family atmosphere. Pastor Gillesby was a handsome 6'3" African-American single man in his late fifties. He lost his wife about eight years ago; however, he had a daughter who was thirty-years-old and served as his administrative assistant at the church, and a son who was thirty-six-years-old. His son was not on staff at the church, but helped out with graphics sometimes when needed for the church. He'd been the pastor of this church for more than twenty or so years and genuinely cared about his congregation, having knowledge of who was a saint and who ain't.

"Amen!" some of the congregation responded. Others were looking around while some were doing what they do best: checking their phones.

Among those scanning through their phones was Calvin, looking handsome as ever. At forty-three, he had grown to about 6'2" and was still a little athletic looking. His hair was cut low and he had a nicely trimmed mustache and goatee. He was dressed in khaki Dockers, a white tailored shirt and a navy blue blazer. He really didn't wear ties to church, but would wear them for work. He was seated with Elaina and their three kids: Katrina, Corey and David. They were all dressed respectably, nothing fancy, but still stylish. They were sedentary with their eyes and ears glued to what Pastor Gillesby was saying as he wrapped up on his sermon.

Calvin was now a project development engineer at a prominent company called Kenner & Welles Inc. with offices in Southfield, Michigan and in Dallas, Texas. Calvin Jr. resided in a sizable five-bedroom home located in an affluent area of Southfield. Elaina was still 5'3" and attractive at forty-two-years-old. She was an English college professor at East Southfield Community College.

Elaina was always striving to apply the same Christian principles to her household that she had growing up. She was not as strict as her parents were with her, but she did try to do her best to live by the Bible and teach their kids to do the same. Perhaps it was this trait that drew her to Calvin, a subtle reminder of his mom and what she tried to do with him.

Their kids had an interesting mixture of personalities and gifts. Katrina was the oldest. She was a beautiful seventeen-year-old who was about 5'2" with long hair; she was a Senior at Montgomery Rose High School. Her desire was to follow in her mother's footsteps and teach. Upon graduation, her plan was to attend University of Florida and enjoy the beaches and sunshine while she was there. Katrina believed she was the boss of her brothers and she made it known to them every chance she got.

Corey, the second oldest, was a humble being, somewhat tall at 5'6" and handsome. He was an intellectual sixteen-year-old fellow who wore glasses. Corey was very devoted to his studies as he desired to be a Cardiologist one day. He was always off to himself, reading all kinds of books, including the Bible; however, he sometimes found time to play video games with his brother. He and David were very close. He had aspirations of attending John Hopkins University when he graduated from Montgomery Rose High School.

And then there was David, the youngest of the three. He was a little on the short side, about 5'4"; however, athletically built and handsome also. He was the comedian of the family or so he believed, and an aspiring pro football player and fanatic. Where Corey kind of kept to himself and was quiet, David had no problem saying what was on his mind. He was fifteen years old and attended the same high school as his sister and brother, playing football there as a running back. His dream was to obtain a football scholarship and be drafted in the NFL.

"God will fight your battles, if you let Him. He loves you very much… more than you know," Pastor Gillesby conveyed to his congregation. "Who will give their lives over to Him today? Notice I said "lives" because I know there are a few out there who need to be up here," Pastor Gillesby asserted as he conducted an altar call while music played softly.

Among the few who were mustering up the courage to stand and go up there was Corey; however, Calvin intercepted by grabbing his arm and asked, "Where are you going?"

"Up there," he told his dad as he pondered why his father was stopping him.

Calvin then asked, "Why?"

Elaina, Katrina and David were all puzzled by Calvin's actions. When he realized what he was doing, he let go of his son's arm.

"I feel I need to, Dad," Corey said and continued to the altar.

David picked up on his brother's courage and stood up also.

Calvin asked, "You too?"

"Calvin, let them go. They need to. Shoot, I pray you will one of these days," Elaina told him with a smirk on her face.

"Shh…" Calvin whispered to his wife.

Elaina gave him her "You better be glad I'm saved!" look, while David joined his brother at the altar. There were a few others up there as well. Pastor Gillesby was very familiar with the Hardy family. Elaina and the kids have been members there for quite a while. When there was a mixture of adults and children at the altar, Pastor Gillesby always gravitated to the children first. He loved when children gave their lives over to the Lord because they were a little bit easier to nurture and lead in the right direction when they were young.

Pastor Gillesby said, "Well, Amen! Who do we have here… the Hardy boys?"

"Yes, sir," said Corey.

"Well, tell the congregation your names and ages." Pastor Gillesby came down with the microphone from the pulpit to where Corey and David were and had them face the congregation. Elaina was all smiles while Calvin, not so much.

"My name is Corey. I'm sixteen."

Then his brother looked at Pastor Gillesby and said, "I'm David. I'm fifteen and need prayer so I can go to the pros, Pastor 'G'. I don't wanna mess your name up, sir."

Pastor Gillesby chuckled at David. "Well, alright young man. For which sport?"

David answered, "Football."

"Well, I'll be sure to do that, David," Pastor Gillesby said, and then focused his attention on Calvin and Elaina. "The Bible says in Proverbs 22:6, Train up a child in the way he should go; even when he is old he will not depart from it," he told them. Then, he put eyes solely on Calvin and said, "Calvin, God holds you responsible for these young men. They need you to be an example of a true Godly man."

Calvin just nodded at him quickly to get the attention off of him.

Pastor Gillesby scanned the congregation, focusing on the men. "I say this to Calvin, but also to every father in here. A father should exemplify leadership built on a biblical foundation and most of all love their children. This world lacks that more than ever. I believe it's mostly due to generational downfalls. Let's be the leaders God called us to be. Amen?"

"Amen!" the congregation as a whole answered.

Pastor Gillesby put his attention back on Corey and David and said, "Now, I want you to always remember, young men... Jesus will never leave nor forsake you, no matter how hard it may get in life. He loves you more than anything. And you can always call on Him when you need Him. Alright?"

"Yes sir," Corey answered.

At the same time, David said, "Alright, Pastor G."

Pastor Gillesby chuckled again at David and said, "Pastor G. I like that, David."

Chapter 6

*T*he ride home from church was a quiet one for Calvin. Not one word came out of his mouth. He got out of his Range Rover and stormed into the house. The rest of his family didn't catch on to his behavior, or maybe it was that they could care less. They walked in seconds later while discussing the service amongst themselves.

Elaina and Katrina followed their normal routine on Sundays after church and headed straight into the kitchen to prepare for dinner. Dinner was usually already done on Sundays after church. Elaina always started her dinner on the night before and finished it up early Sunday morning before church. So all she had to do after service was just warm up the food while Katrina set the table with plates, napkins, glasses and silverware. On Sundays, the guys always had the privilege of just coming into the house, changing into comfortable clothes and coming to the table hungry.

The kitchen was very spacious and included an island. It also had a bay window where a dark wooden table with six cushioned chairs sat. There was a formal dining area right outside of the kitchen; however, it was only used for special occasions. Elaina had the oven on and stove piping hot so that it would only take a few moments to heat up the food. And the meal wouldn't be complete without some kind of dessert. Sometimes it was homemade and sometimes not. On this day, it was a Mrs. Smith's flaky crust dutch apple pie which Elaina had in the oven baking already. Now that the table was set and the food was heating, Elaina and Katrina quickly changed clothes, then returned to the kitchen to begin placing the food on the table. Elaina dressed a large bowl with sliced roast and gravy, and then filled up two bowls with mashed potatoes and green beans while Katrina arranged some buttered dinner rolls on a plate. Elaina had also made a pitcher of fresh lemonade which was sitting on the kitchen counter. The countertops were all granite in a black, beige and coral pattern.

Elaina yelled to Calvin and the boys, "Come on, guys! Time to eat!" not knowing her husband was already heading to the kitchen.

He entered into the kitchen, grabbed his glass sitting by his plate, and opened the fridge looking inside.

Elaina took notice as she stood by the sink and said, "I made some lemonade if you want some. It's over here on the counter." He slammed the fridge door. Elaina noticed that too, but didn't say a word to him. Still without word and a frown on his face, Calvin walked over to the counter and poured himself some lemonade, then took his seat at the table and began fixing his plate. Katrina was already sitting at the table just waiting for everyone else. Her plate was already fixed. Corey and David finally showed up to the kitchen, got their drinks, and took their seats at the table along with Elaina, before they began loading their plates with food. There were no special seating assignments for the kitchen table; just whoever got there first, with the exception of Calvin. His seat was always at the head of the table, on either end. Elaina would just sit on either side of him.

Elaina quickly said to Calvin as she looked at David, "Honey, can you go ahead and bless the food before everyone starts eating?" She'd caught David trying to sneak the first bite of his food.

David quickly bowed his head while his brother and sister snickered.

Calvin responded, "You can go ahead and do it today."

Elaina was taken by his response. He always said the grace for Sunday's dinner. She replied, "Okay…" wondering why he didn't want to say it. She just went on ahead and said it herself. "Lord, thank you for today and for what took place with Corey and David. We ask that you bless our family and this food. Amen."

Everyone began stuffing their faces, except Elaina. She fixed her eyes on Calvin for a moment, as she was still wondering why his face displayed a scowl as if he were mad at the world. She proceeded to fix her food and began eating. But after a while, she just couldn't take his foul look anymore and said, "Well, what's your problem? Today is supposed to be a celebration."

Calvin answered, "A celebration for what, Laina? My sons being drawn into hypocrisy?"

"Everyone in the church are not hypocrites, Calvin. And every man in the church is not your dad. What, are you afraid your sons will turn out to be like him because they went to the altar?"

"No," he told her. "I just don't trust churches. It didn't help my dad, and he was a deacon."

"Well, why do you even go, Calvin, if you don't like church?"

Calvin responded, "To make sure no other guy has his eye on you."

"You're kidding, right?" she asked, with a slight smirk on her face.

Their kids were bouncing their heads back and forth between their parents as they ate and listened to their parents' conversation.

"No, I'm not," he told her.

"Well, let me assure you there are no worries on that. As far as your dad, he must not have had as close relationship with God as he tried to portray. And when you don't, you open yourself up to anything wrong. Trust me… been there, done that… way before you came into the picture. The only way you won't become him or do what he did, is do what the boys did today… get close to God. Without him, the devil is going to make sure you become your dad."

"Not in a million years!" he told her blatantly.

"Well babe, I know you can't hate the church or your dad for that matter, forever. 'Cause in the end, that," she pointed to the left side of his chest, "needs to be right with God."

Calvin asked, "Oh, you're a preacher now, Laina?"

She chuckled, then told him, "Not at all, Calvin. I'm just telling you what I know."

"Dad, nobody in the church made me go up there today. I can't explain it, but it was like I heard a voice saying to go," Corey told his dad. Elaina nodded.

"And David, why did you go up there?" asked Elaina.

David answered proudly, "Because my brother went up there. And I'm glad I did."

"Why is that?" Calvin asked.

"Cause Pastor G is gone pray for me that I go to the pros."

Calvin asked, "You think a preacher is going to help you get to the pros, David?"

"No, but his prayers can. And since I followed Corey up there, my chances are high. He's the smart one out of us," said David, as he glanced, with a silly smirk on his face, over at Katrina.

Katrina returned to him a mean look.

"Well, I hope you're right, David, because prayer didn't work for me," Calvin told him.

"Why you say that, Daddy?" he asked.

"It just didn't. Trust me. If it did, we'd be living in a much bigger home and then maybe I could have experienced that." He pointed to a Sports Illustrated magazine sitting on the table by David.

His dad knew David had brought it in there even though he shouldn't have, but didn't say anything because he was in a mood. 'Super Bowl' was written on the cover. David had it in his hand when he came into the kitchen and was just too lazy to take it back to his bedroom. Elaina didn't realize it was on the table until Calvin pointed at it.

Elaina asked David, "What is that doing at the table?"

He quickly took the magazine off of the table and dropped it on the floor.

"You played football, Daddy? You never mentioned that," said David.

"Yeah, because it was nothing to talk about."

"Why, what happened?" David asked, not knowing that he was adding fire to the fuel.

"My dad didn't have time for it... that's what happened. The man was always gone. Always claimed to be at church when he really wasn't."

David asked, "Where was he?"

Elaina just dropped her head down and said to herself, "Oh, Lord..."

Calvin responded, "Not with me or your grandmother! At one of the church lady's house."

"So, that's why you don't like church," David told him.

"That's why I don't trust church people. And now, look like they've sucked you two in," said Calvin.

"Lord, this man," Elaina said underneath her breath, as she looked toward the ceiling. "Calvin, I'm telling you... If you don't learn to forgive your dad, that unforgiveness is going to be used as fuel to destroy you."

Calvin said, "Laina, I'll never forgive my dad for what he did. He don't deserve it!"

"Well, when did you become God? Do you know He could say the same thing about you, but He doesn't? You're only hurting yourself by carrying around all this anger and

51

bitterness against him. And you're dragging us in with you whether you realize it or not… every time we go to church, anytime we mention church, and God forbid, if we ask questions about him," Elaina said.

"I'm not dragging you guys in."

Elaina murmured, "Hmm."

"Hmm, what? He was dead to me back then and he's dead to me now," said Calvin. He cleaned his mouth off with a napkin and stood up from the table. "I'll be back in a little while. I'm going to meet up with T.B. He's in town from Dallas."

"Oh, really?" said Elaina.

It was true T.B. was in town, however; Calvin was just ready to escape their conversation. "Yeah, he is."

Elaina replied, "Well, tell him I said hey."

"Alright," Calvin said. He left out of the kitchen and out of the front door.

Corey said, "Wow, Mom… Dad is really angry with his dad."

"Yeah, he is Corey. Still after forty some years. We just need to pray for him. He's just so stubborn."

Chapter 7

Calvin opened the door, scouting for his childhood friend, Tony Brown at a place called Jay's Lounge, a small bar located near the area where they lived growing up. He and T.B. hung out there sometimes, for drinks. It was a rather pleasant and friendly atmosphere and had been renovated since their college days. They'd added a stage for entertainment, but no one was performing at the moment. However, soothing jazz played and the lights were somewhat muted. It was a good little crowd for a Sunday afternoon. Half of the tables were filled with patrons, and some were sitting at the bar, keeping the bartender busy. It was a mixture of different ethnic backgrounds, but mostly African-American.

After a careful scan of the room, Calvin took notice of his best pal sitting with his back slightly turned toward the entrance at a table near a wall, close to the other side of the building. He approached his table.

Once at his table, he stood behind T.B. and said, "Never has been one to miss out on happy hour, huh T.B.?"

Tony turned around, stood up and gave Calvin dap and a manly embrace. "C.J., what's up?"

"You! It looks like Dallas been treating you good, man. You here visiting your parents?"

"Yeah, man, you know that's all I come back to Southfield for."

Calvin took a quick glance at Tony's left hand and said, "And I see you're not married yet."

"Now, you know you would be the first to know. Who else would be my best man? And man, I'm still waiting for the right one."

"What, one that has long hair and a coke bottle shape?" asked Calvin.

Tony laughed. "Naw, man... maybe in the past," he told him. "I'm looking for one who loves God like I do. And of course, long hair and a coke bottle shape along with that won't hurt," Tony said with a quick raise of his eyebrows.

They both laughed.

"So, you a church man now, T.B.?"

"I wouldn't call myself a church man. Just that I'm not the same man you've known in the past. I live now for the man upstairs."

"So, how did the preacher reel you in?" Calvin asked.

"Well, he talked some. And I listened, but I decided to make that change myself, C.J."

Calvin replied with a slight smile, "And I guess you live without sin now."

"I didn't say that. Nobody's perfect, C.J. That's why we need God... to put us in check sometimes. You know how that is."

"Yeah, yeah. I hear ya," Calvin said. "Did you and my wife talk to each other before I came here?"

"No, why?" Tony asked.

"She's been talking about God and how I should forgive my dad. I'm just not hearing that right now. You remember that, T.B.?"

"Yeah, I do. I really felt bad for you on that day, man... but your wife is right. You gotta find a way to forgive him," Tony told him. "So that's why all the questions. I'm gone get Laina for bringing all the heat to me."

"Oh, and she told me to tell you hey, too."

Tony replied, "Tell my sister I said hey, and give her a kiss on the cheek from me."

"I'll tell her. The kiss on the cheek from you, though, I'll have to think about," Calvin told him with a sly grin.

Tony laughed as he looked at his empty glass. "Let me go get a refill on my drink. You want something?"

"Yeah, I'll take whatever you're drinking. I can't stay too much longer, or I'll have to hear it from Laina. You know her."

"Yeah, I do," Tony said. "Alright, be right back." He walked over to the bar and waited patiently until a beautiful fair-skinned African-American woman in her early thirties who was sitting at the bar, got her drink from the bartender. She had long hair and was dressed cute, wearing some casual pants and a fashionable top. She didn't go unnoticed by Tony.

The bartender slid her drink to her and said, "Here's your dirty martini, ma'am." The woman stayed at the bar, sipping on her dirty martini while the bartender obtained Tony's request.

"What can I get for you?"

"Yeah, I need another Coke, please. And actually make that two," he told the bartender.

"You got it."

Moments after his order was taken, the woman at the bar turned toward Tony to get down from the stool and ended up hitting his arm with the hand she held her drink, spilling it on his shirt.

"I am so sorry," she told Tony. "Here... let me grab some napkins." She grabbed a few napkins from the bar and wiped his shirt. "I didn't realize I was that close to you."

"That's okay. I'll get it," he told her. Tony grabbed a few more napkins from the bar and wiped his shirt, too.

The woman felt bad that Tony was cleaning his shirt and said, "I really am sorry. I wasn't paying attention. I've had a long week."

"I understand. Really... it's not a problem," he told her with an inviting smile. The bartender placed both of Tony's drinks down in front of him; however, he was still engaged in conversation with the woman. "You come here a lot?" asked Tony.

"No, I'm here on a business trip and thought I would try this place out."

"Well, you picked a good spot. My buddy and I came here often when I lived here."

"Oh, you don't live here anymore?" she asked.

"No. My parents still do. I'm here visiting them."

The bartender, who saw what happened, handed the woman another dirty martini.

"Thank you," she told the bartender.

"So, what's your name?" asked Tony.

"It's Patrice. Patrice Nelson."

"Well Patrice, I'm Tony. Tony Brown." Tony shook her hand and asked, "You wanna join us at our table?" Tony pointed at his and Calvin's table.

"Oh, I don't wanna intrude on you guys," Patrice said.

"You won't be intruding. I'm sure my friend won't mind. He's married anyway. I'm not," he replied with a smile. He finally picked up the two drinks he ordered.

"Well okay, sure." Patrice followed Tony back to the table. He sat Calvin's drink in front of him and put his down where he'd been sitting.

"C.J., this is Patrice Nelson. She's here on a business trip. I told her she can join us."

"Yeah, sure," Calvin said. "I'll be leaving soon anyway." He sipped on his drink while Tony and Patrice sat down. "T.B., I thought you were getting me what you were drinking? This is just Coke. What happened to the rum part?"

Tony responded, "You're drinking what I was drinking."

"Wow, I guess you have changed," said Calvin.

Tony grinned. "So Patrice, how long are you in town for?" Tony asked.

"Only for another week."

He asked, "What do you do for a living, if you don't mind me asking?"

"I'm an Internal Auditor."

"Wow, that's sounds big time," said Tony.

Calvin intervened saying, "That is big time."

"I don't know about that... I know it's a lot of work," Patrice said.

"I hear you. So, where is home for you?" Tony asked her.

"In Dallas."

"You're kidding?" Tony said, trying not to show too much excitement.

"No, why?"

Calvin intervened again with, "Because that's where Tony lives now."

"Wow, really?"

"Yep," confirmed Tony.

Calvin drank the last bit of Coke in his glass, then stood up and said, "Well, I better get out of here, T.B. before Laina starts calling." Tony stood up and gave Calvin dap and that manly embrace again. "Good seeing you again, man. Patrice, it was nice meeting you," said Calvin. He asked Patrice, "You go to church?"

"Yeah, I do, when I'm home," she replied.

Calvin smiled and nodded his head at Tony. Tony knew exactly why.

"I'll talk to you later, T.B. Enjoy Patrice's company. Sounds like you two have a couple of things in common."

"Alright, man. We'll talk later," Tony told him, and Calvin left the bar.

Chapter 8

"**Y**ou're back. You want some dessert?" Elaina asked Calvin as he entered into the kitchen. She was sitting at the kitchen table by her lonesome, enjoying a slice of the Mrs. Smith's apple pie she baked earlier. The whole pie was sitting on the table.

Calvin quickly responded, "Yeah, I'll take some," and joined Elaina at the table.

With a mouthful of pie, Elaina got up and grabbed a dessert plate from the ones sitting on the counter, then cut a slice for her husband and served it to him before taking her seat.

"So, how's T.B. doing these days?" Elaina asked.

"Well, he said he loves Dallas. He's not married yet… says he's waiting for the right one."

"And what's the right one?"

"One who loves God," Calvin said with sarcasm.

"Well, Amen!"

"Oh, I knew *you* would love that. And he told me to tell you hey and to give you a kiss on the cheek."

"Well?"

"Well what?" asked Calvin.

Elaina replied, "You didn't give me the kiss on the cheek."

"I didn't tell him I would do it. I told him I'd think about it. I thought about it, and decided not to give you a kiss from him," Calvin told her. "I don't want no other man sending a kiss to you... even if it is through me."

Elaina smiled and shook her head.

She said, "C.J., you are something else."

Suddenly, the doorbell rang as Corey and David were entering into the kitchen. Their parents already knew what they were coming for.

"I'll get it," said Elaina. She was done with her pie, so she didn't mind getting up again.

Now Corey and David was coming in to devour some apple pie, too. They grabbed dessert plates off of the counter, cut themselves a huge slice of pie, and joined their dad at the table.

At the front door, Elaina took a glimpse through the peep hole. It was Darren Border, someone Elaina called brother. He was an attractive, clean cut, average height African-American man in his early forties who was the youth director at a Southfield Neighborhood Community Center.

He'd been the director there for at least ten years or more. Elaina's mother, Momma James, was a good friend of Darren's mother. They didn't live far from Elaina's childhood home. And Darren also went to school with Elaina and her sister. Everyone knew him as their big brother because he would always take up for them, as if they needed it. Momma James' girls were bold at the mouth, rough and tough.

When Darren was ten, he lost his mother to illness and unfortunately, never knew his father. So, his grandparents took over caring for him; however, when his mother was alive and even after her death, he would always come over to Momma and Papa James house to eat dinner. That's what he called them. Although on Sundays, he couldn't eat dinner at their home unless he went to church with them. That was Momma James' rule. And let's just say, Darren didn't miss a lot of her Sunday meals; he attended church with them frequently.

"Well, I should have known. Did you smell the food from your place, Darren?" Elaina asked as she opened the door.

"Very funny, Laina." He followed Elaina to the kitchen. Calvin, Corey and David were still at the table chomping down on their apple pie. "What's up everybody? Any leftovers?" Darren asked. Some things just didn't change.

62

"Man, do you ever cook?" asked Calvin.

Corey and David snickered.

Elaina intervened and replied, "Yes, Darren, we have some food left. I'll fix you a plate." Elaina grabbed a dinner plate and loaded it up with roast, mashed potatoes, green beans and a couple of dinner rolls.

Darren took a seat at the table with the men. "Thank ya, Sis," he told Elaina. "And yes, C.J., I do cook... Stouffer's, Banquet and Ramen noodles."

Everyone snickered. Elaina placed the plate of food in front of him along with a glass of lemonade.

"And I see apple pie! Looks like Mrs. Smith's flaky crust dutch apple pie. Let me hurry up and eat this so I can get me some of that," said Darren.

Elaina, Corey and David laughed at him while Calvin just shook his head as Darren gulped his food down.

"Uncle Darren, are we able to come up to the center sometimes?" David asked.

"Yeah, anytime. Well, not during school of course, but after school if it's alright with your parents."

"David, how are you going to be able to go? You have football practice all the time," Corey said.

"I know, but maybe I can go when the season is over."

"Yeah, you can't miss out on practice if you're talking about going to the pros. I don't think you're gonna be

63

big enough anyway for the pros, but who knows," Calvin told him.

"Well, wait a minute, C.J... they're some great guys in the pros who're small," Darren interjected while yet stuffing his face. "There's Ray Rice and Darren Sproles!"

"Yeah, I know. But David needs a lot of work to get to their level."

"So, why don't you help him, Dad?" suggested Corey. "Since you didn't get a chance to play like you wanted to, you can live vicariously through David," Corey explained with a smile.

Elaina came over from washing dishes and laid her hand on Corey's shoulder and told him, "That's an excellent idea, Corey." She stood there for a moment to see what Calvin's response was going to be. As a matter of fact, all eyes were on him.

Calvin replied, "I'll think about it."

Elaina gave an unpleasant smirk on her face and went back to washing the dishes.

"Since that matter is *somewhat* settled, can *I* go to the center after school?" asked Corey.

Calvin replied, "If it's okay with your mom, it's fine with me."

Elaina nodded in agreement as she continued working on cleaning the dishes. "I'll pick you up on my way home from work, Corey. Just be ready," said Calvin.

"I will."

"I can bring him home sometimes too, C.J., if you need me to," said Darren.

"Well, the center is on the way here. So, I should be fine picking him up."

"And David since you can't come yet, maybe you and your brother can come with me when I take the guys to see NBA and NFL games. I'm sure you would rather go see a football game though, right?"

David's ears began to perk up.

"Yezzir!" he answered.

"I already knew the answer to that," Darren said, as he wiped his mouth with a napkin after eating every bit of food off of his plate. "Well, I better get out of here. Laina, if you don't mind, I'll take my apple pie to go."

"Alright," she said as she looked strangely at his plate. "I'll wrap up a piece for you."

"Thank you. And as always Sis, the food was delicious."

Elaina replied, "Really? I couldn't tell." Then shook her head while smiling. Darren's plate was completely clean without any trace of food on it. He pushed back from the table and rubbed his stomach.

"Well Laina, you won't have to wash his plate. He took care of that for you with his mouth," Calvin said.

Darren laughed slightly as he stood up from the table and said, "Whatever man. Well, I'll see y'all later." He yelled "Bye Trina!"

She was in her bedroom doing what most teenage girls do, on her phone gabbing.

She yelled back, "Bye, Uncle Darren!"

"See you later, Darren," Elaina said and handed him his wrapped up apple pie as he left out of the kitchen and out of the front door.

"Daddy, can you start helping me next Saturday with football?" David asked. He figured if he asked his dad again, he would go ahead and just say yes.

"It will have to be the following Saturday, David. I actually wanted to see if you guys wanted to go to my company's fall festival this coming Saturday?" He asked them.

David asked, "Any girls gone be there?"

"Right," Corey said, backing up his brother. Corey was into his books and David was into his football, but they both were still fascinated with girls.

Calvin smiled, answering, "I don't know."

Katrina finally took a break from gabbing and came into the kitchen. She asked, "What are you guys talking about?"

Elaina replied, "Your dad wanted to know if we would like to go to his company's fall festival on this Saturday."

"Yeah, I'm in. Wait… are any guys my age gone be there?" Katrina asked.

"Now, there you go," Calvin said while her brothers laughed.

"What? I'm just asking," said Katrina.

Elaina just shook her head and smiled.

Chapter 9

"*I*'ve got to do something with this hair," Patrice said to herself as she looked in the mirror in the bathroom at her corporate apartment in Southfield. She picked through her frizzy hair and said to herself, "I hope it wasn't like this in front of Tony." Her hair was hanging down with fallen curls. She had changed out of the clothes she had on at Jay's Lounge into something more relaxing. She took the hair scrunchy that was sitting on the sink by her cell phone and pulled her hair up in it. Then, she grabbed her cell phone and called her hair stylist, April, a pretty African-American woman in her early thirties who was located in Dallas, Texas.

"Hey, Patrice."

"April, hey. Do you happen to know of a hair stylist here in Southfield, Michigan?" Patrice asked. "The humidity here has been brutal on my hair and I could use a quick touch up. I have a date, girl!"

April chuckled and said, "Umm… aren't you supposed to be there working?"

"I am, but I need a little pleasure, too."

April smiled as she nodded on the other end and said, "I gotcha. And yeah, I know someone."

"I figured you would. You know everybody everywhere that has something to do with hair," Patrice said.

"There's a salon called Elegance Beyond owned by a friend of mine named Michelle. She'll do it for you."

"Okay, great! Let me grab something so I can write her number down." Patrice grabbed a notepad off of a small table right outside of the bathroom. "Okay, go ahead with the number."

"Her number is 248-555-9988. I'll call her and let her know you're going to be calling."

"Okay, thank you. I'll give her a call first thing in the morning. See you when I get back," said Patrice.

April responded, "Alright, girl. Enjoy your date."

Moments later after hanging up with April, Patrice's cell phone rang. She didn't recognize the number that popped up, but answered it anyway. "Hello?"

"Patrice, this is Tony."

"Oh, hey Tony." She walked over to the sofa and positioned herself comfortably while she chatted.

"I hope you don't mind me calling you so soon, but just wanted to tell you that I really enjoyed talking with you today, and I'm looking forward to seeing you again."

"Yeah, I enjoyed it, too. Even though I messed up your shirt," she told him. "I felt so stupid."

Tony replied, "No, no, don't worry about it. I would've never met you if that didn't happen. So, I think it was fate."

Patrice chuckled and said, "I guess. If that's what you wanna call it. I call it being clumsy and embarrassing."

"Naw, it's all good. I promise," he told her. "Well, I know it's late and I wanna be able to continue earning your respect and attention, so I'm gonna let you go and get some rest."

"Yeah, I am a little tired," said Patrice. "So, I'll see you tomorrow night at seven, right?"

"On the dot."

"Great. Well you have a good night, Tony."

"You too, Patrice." They both smiled as they hung up; Tony's much bigger however, as he celebrated with himself.

Chapter 10

*P*atrice had her hair pulled up into a scrunchy, wearing active wear clothing and sunglasses on as she entered into a sophisticated hair salon called Elegance Beyond owned and operated by a pretty African-American woman in her early thirties named Michelle. It was a relaxing atmosphere with only a few patrons getting their hair done on that afternoon. Two were under the dryer, while two were in a stylist chair. There were three hairstylists who did hair in the salon, including Michelle. While Michelle was sweeping hair up from around her chair, she noticed Patrice at the front desk and approached her.

"Are you Patrice?"

"Yes. You're Michelle?"

"I am."

"Thank you for getting me in so quickly," Patrice told her. "I was telling April that the humidity has been brutal on my hair. But I will say, it's worse in Dallas than it is here."

"Yeah, I know. Well, I'm just glad I could help out on short notice. And you came at the right time, when it's not as busy," Michelle said. "You can have a seat in my chair over there." She pointed to her chair and Patrice walked over to it with Michelle following behind her. "So, you're just here for business?" she asked as she began taking Patrice's hair down out of the scrunchy to inspect it.

Patrice said, "Yeah, just for one more week. I come here for two weeks out of each month for work. I may need to grab you as my permanent hair stylist when I come to town."

"Yeah, sure. We don't turn down any clients whether you live out of town, in town, up town or down town for that matter. As long you have the money to pay for your services."

Patrice chuckled, then asked, "How do you know April?"

"I met April some years ago at a hair show in Detroit. And we've been close friends since then."

"I told her she knows just about everyone in the hair business."

"Yeah, she does. Well, follow me to the wash bowl and we'll get you fixed up. Your hair doesn't look all that bad," Michelle said while they walked to the wash bowl.

Patrice replied, "Well, I don't know about that. I just need it to look nice for a date I have tonight, and then an outing on Saturday."

"So, sounds like to me, you aiming to look cute all week long," Michelle said smiling.

Patrice said, "Yeah... basically," then sat down at the wash bowl.

Michelle began to wash her hair. "Well, hopefully what we do today will last until Saturday," said Michelle.

"I sure hope so. I'll just have to make sure I take care of it during the week."

"Not trying to be nosey or anything, but what'd you doing on Saturday?" Michelle asked, being nosey.

"Oh, that's okay. I'm going to spend the day with this guy I met. That's who my date is with tonight."

"Say no more," Michelle said. "Let me go ahead and hook you up, girl."

Chapter 11

Although there was a slight nip in the air, the sun was still bringing forth it's warmth on this November day at Beech Woods Park. The air was filled with the smell of popcorn, cotton candy, corn dogs, turkey legs, funnel cakes… you name it. And there were people of all ages roaming about eating, playing games or on a ride if they were young enough. There were only a few rides which were for small children; however, plenty of games and food for everyone. Kenner & Welles Inc. made sure of that.

Calvin along with Elaina, Katrina, Corey and David were strolling around together, taking in the sights. He caught a glimpse of his boss, Simon Talarskew, a Caucasian man in his early to mid-fifties and his wife, Pamela, a Caucasian bubbly woman in her late forties, standing near the balloon dart board game looking around.

Calvin said, "I see my boss. Let me introduce you guys to him and his wife." Then he and his family walked over to Simon and Pamela. Elaina and the kids stood behind Calvin once he reached his boss.

"Calvin! So glad you and your family could make it," said Simon. He turned to his wife and said, "This is my wife, Pamela."

Pamela shook Calvin's hand as she spoke and said, "Pleasure to meet you, Calvin. Simon says you're a great engineer."

"I'd like to think so. Oh, let me introduce you to my family," he told Simon and Pamela.

"You all… this is my boss, Simon Talarskew and his wife, Pamela."

Elaina shook Simon's and Pamela's hand as she spoke. "Nice to meet you," Elaina said.

"And please… call me Pam. So good to meet you, Elaina."

"Likewise."

"And these are our children, Katrina, Corey and David," Calvin told Simon and Pam.

"Hi," said Katrina.

"Hello," Corey said.

"Nice to meet you, Mr. Ta-lars—," David attempted to pronounce Simon's last name, but was struggling.

His brother interrupted and murmured, "Mmm, mmm…" while shaking his head. He was trying to keep him from embarrassing himself. Katrina turned her head away and chuckled.

David said quickly, "Nice to meet you, sir."

"That's okay, David. I have people I've worked with for many years who still can't say my last name," said Simon. "Well, there's plenty to enjoy around here. Help yourself. You all excuse us for a moment. We're going to go greet some other folks," Simon told Calvin and his family. He and his wife walked off.

And moments later, Katrina, Corey and David abandoned their parents as well to go do their own thing. Not long after their kids left, Elaina turned around in the same direction as the kids and recognized what she believed was a familiar face standing not too far off at some kind of game station.

Elaina said, "Calvin, is that T.B.?"

"Where?"

"Over there," Elaina said as she pointed in that direction.

Calvin fixed his eyes over that way to see if he recognized his friend.

"Yeah, I think that is his noggin. I wonder what he's doing here?"

"And who's the woman with him?" Elaina wondered. The woman's back was turned toward Calvin and Elaina.

"I'm not sure. Let's go find out," Calvin said as he and Elaina proceeded over to them. "What's up T.B.?" Calvin said.

Surprised at the voice behind him, T.B. and the woman quickly turned around. "And Patrice?" Calvin said. Now he was really curious as to why they were at the festival.

Her hair, full of curls, was down and she had on light colored skinny jeans and a cardigan sweater over a top that complemented her sweater. Patrice eyed Calvin quickly from head to toe. He was dressed in some nice dark blue jeans with a sky blue long sleeved collar shirt and a dark brown leather belt that matched his loafers. His wife was dressed just as fashionable as she had on a cute long sleeve fall top, dark blue jeans and dark brown boots that came up just below the knee. However, her attire didn't seem to get Patrice's attention as much as Calvin's did.

Elaina took notice of the attention that Patrice gave her husband, and she began mulling over how Calvin knew this Patrice woman.

Calvin asked, "What are you guys doing here?"

"Well, after you left Jay's, Patrice told me who she worked for and it happened to be for your company. She was the one who told me about the festival and invited me to come," T.B. told Calvin. "I was planning on surprising you, but I guess that didn't work," he said with a smirk.

"So, Patrice you do internal auditing for us?" asked Calvin.

"That's right. I spend two weeks out of each month here."

Elaina interrupted and said, "Umm, hello? Is anybody going to introduce me?" She wanted to make sure Patrice knew that she was his wife.

"I'm sorry, Laina. This is Patrice Nelson. I met her at Jay's... by accident when she spilled her drink on me last Sunday," Tony told Elaina as he laughed slightly. He said, "Patrice, this is Elaina, Calvin's wife."

"So Calvin, how do you know Patrice?" Elaina asked her husband, not wasting any time to find out *their* acquaintance.

Calvin quickly responded, "I met her at Jay's also when T.B. invited her to our table."

"Oh, okay. He didn't tell me all of that," Elaina said as she made eye contact with Calvin.

Calvin knew exactly what she was thinking, which was, 'Why didn't you tell me all of this?'.

Elaina turned to Patrice and said, "Well, nice to meet you, Patrice."

"You too, Elaina."

"Well, I guess T.B. will be spending time between Dallas and here," said Calvin.

"Just maybe," Tony stated, as his eyes locked in on Patrice.

"So T.B., did you stay here for another week?" asked Calvin.

"No, I left on Tuesday and then came back here on yesterday. I'm leaving tomorrow to go back to Dallas, though."

"Yeah, me too," Patrice said.

Elaina intervened with, "Well, how about right now, we all get something to eat? All this standing around trying to figure out who's who and who's leaving or staying, has me starving."

"Sounds like a great idea, Elaina," Patrice told her. They all walked off together, heading to toward the food area.

Chapter 12

"*P*atrice… what are you still doing here?" Calvin asked, when he noticed her walking in the hallway past the glass window of his office at Kenner & Welles Inc. He ceased from reviewing some documents and quickly got up, peeking out of his office to get her attention. He was dressed in a sharp navy blue suit with a white collar shirt and complementing tie. He had a moderate sized office with a nice maple wood desk. There were two chairs that sat in front of his desk. On his desk was a computer, a desk phone, a large desk calendar along with scattered papers and a couple of framed family pictures. Behind where Calvin sat, was a large window that looked out into downtown Southfield.

Kenner & Welles Inc. was in a ten story glass window building that employed about 15,000 people between the Southfield and Dallas offices. They oversaw the building of business and housing development projects.

"Oh, hey, Calvin. I had an unexpected meeting early this morning. I actually leave out in a couple hours to go back to Dallas," Patrice said. She had on a black pencil skirt with a tan long sleeve silk blouse, matching pumps and lovely jewelry that complemented her outfit.

"Oh, okay," replied Calvin.

"I'm headed to the cafeteria. You want me to get you something?" she asked him. "It's the least I can do for ruining you and Tony's male bonding time."

Calvin took a quick glance at his watch to see what time it was, and said, "Well, I haven't had anything to eat yet for lunch. Why don't I join you, if you're okay with that? Then you won't have to eat by yourself."

"Yeah, sounds good. And you can fill me in on the stuff I don't know about Tony."

"Okay, yeah. That's my boy." Calvin closed the door to his office and headed to the cafeteria with Patrice. When they arrived at the cafeteria, they both grabbed a tray, selected the food items they wanted, and found a table. The cafeteria was large and set up like a bistro. It was always full of people during breakfast and lunch time. Patrice had a large grilled chicken caesar salad and drink on her tray, while Calvin had a steak sandwich, fries and drink on his.

"So how long have you worked for Kenner & Welles?" asked Calvin.

"For about three years."

"That's strange; I've never seen you here before."

"Yeah, I've never seen you either. Unless I've seen you in passing and just never paid any attention to you."

81

Calvin replied, "Wow, thanks, Patrice."

"No, I didn't mean in that way," Patrice said. "I'm so busy when I'm here that I don't really have time to take notice of who works here," she explained. "You ever been to the Dallas office?"

"No, I haven't, but I hear it's really nice. And actually, I think we're getting ready to begin some business developments there."

"Yeah, I think you're right. Will you be working on any of those?"

"I don't know, but I may ask my boss about it. It'll give me a chance to check out the Dallas office and hang with Tony while I'm there."

"Yeah, you should," Patrice said. "So, how long have you been married, Calvin?"

"For seventeen years." Calvin stuffed his mouth with fries.

"Wow, that's a long time. You don't ever get tired of being married for that long?"

Calvin answered proudly, "No, not really. I love my wife."

"Well, I hope I can have that one day. Elaina is really lucky to have you," she said with a smile before looking at her watch. "I better get going so I can make it to the airport on time."

"I can drop you off. I'm just about done wrapping up on some things. Can you wait about fifteen minutes?"

"Well, I was going to take a cab. Are you sure it won't put you out of the way?"

"No, it won't. I have to pick up my son, but I'll be there in time." Just as Calvin got ready to take a bite of his steak sandwich, he noticed he had gotten ketchup all over one of his cuff links. "Shoot!"

"What? You just remembered you have to do something else?" asked Patrice.

"No, no. I got ketchup all over my cuff link," he told Patrice while taking it off. He went ahead and took the other one off to check it as well. "T.B. had these made for me for my wedding." He wiped them both off before showing Patrice. The links were engraved with a capital 'C' and an emerald in the middle of the 'C'. Calvin sat them off to the side of the table. Patrice picked up one of them to take a closer look.

"They're beautiful. Does the emerald mean anything?"

"That's my birthstone."

"Aww, that was nice of Tony." She put the cuff link back with the other one. "So you're a May man."

"Yes, I'm a May man," said Calvin.

Patrice checked her watch again. "Now, Calvin, are you sure I won't be inconveniencing you?"

"No, not at all." He stood up and grabbed his tray. There wasn't much left on his plate. "I guess I need to go ahead and wrap things up so I can get you to the airport on time."

"I'll wait for you here," she told him. "And you know, you didn't give me any info on Tony."

Calvin said, "You didn't ask for any. Give me a few moments. I'll be right back." He quickly headed out of the cafeteria after dumping his tray.

Patrice noticed that he had left his cuff links on the table and she put them inside her purse before she dumped her tray. She walked back to where she'd been sitting and sat back down, looking around the cafeteria while she waited for Calvin. Shortly after, Calvin came back in to get her and they headed to the airport.

Calvin pulled up to the Delta Airlines drop off lane and stepped out of his Range Rover to help Patrice with her luggage. He sat her luggage in front of her.

"Calvin, thank you so much for this."

"Oh, no problem. Glad I could help. And keep Tony in line for me," he told her.

"I will." She smiled and gave Calvin a hug.

He didn't hug her back at first because he wasn't expecting that, but then returned a hug loosely.

"Thanks again," she said before heading into the building.

Calvin stood there for a moment to watch as she walked in, and then hopped back in his truck, leaving the airport.

Chapter 13

*T*he Southfield Neighborhood Community Center was full of girls and boys of various ages and ethnicities, roaming throughout the center, playing checkers, ping-pong, jumping rope, sitting at tables doing homework, or in huddles talking to each other. There were also a few adult workers, both men and women, walking around monitoring the children's activities. It was a huge spacious center with a gym on the inside, classrooms, meeting rooms and a little area where the kids could just chill. And outside were picnic tables, a basketball court and a rugged looking football field where they held youth football league games.

Corey was tucked away in a corner playing ping-pong with another teen boy around his age, when Darren and a teen named Kenny, approached the ping-pong table to check out the game.

"So who's got this game?" asked Darren.

"Must you ask, Uncle Darren? You know I'm the ping-pong king around here."

"That's what I hear. I'll have to see for myself. I'm gone have to bring you over to the house for a couple of games, and then we'll see."

"Alright, sure," Corey said.

"Well guys, I'll see you tomorrow. I have to make a post office run before I drop Kenny off at home. Make sure all your homework is done before you leave." Kenny, for some reason, had a look of discontent that didn't go unnoticed.

Corey replied, "Already done, Uncle Darren." Darren and Kenny headed out of the center while Corey and his opponent ended their game. "I wonder what was wrong with Kenny?" asked Corey. His opponent shrugged his shoulders. Moments later, Corey looked outside and saw his dad pulling up. He knew he would be soon. "Hey, better luck next time, man. There's my dad. Later," he told his opponent, and picked up this book bag that was leaning against the ping-pong table, before heading out the door. Corey won the game and hadn't lost against an opponent since he'd been coming to the center. He opened the passenger side of his dad's truck and got in the front seat. "Hey, Dad."

Calvin said, "What's up, Corey? How was your day?" Calvin backed out.

"Good," answered Corey while looking at his dad strangely. "You sure are in a good mood."

"Why you say that?" Calvin asked.

"Because you never ask how my day was. Normally, you have that 'It's been a long day.' look on your face," he told his dad. Then asked, "Was your day good?"

"My day was great!"

"How, what happened?"

"I…" Calvin thought to himself, 'Maybe I shouldn't tell him about Patrice.' So he answered, "Got a lot done today in a short amount of time."

"Oh okay, cool, Dad. That's always a plus," Corey told him. "I got a lot done today, too, in a short amount of time."

"Oh, yeah? What did you have to do?"

"Well, I didn't have to do it, but I thrashed a few opponents in ping-pong games, in a short amount of time." Calvin laughed.

"So, I take it you like coming to the center?"

"Yes, I do. Uncle Darren does pretty well running that place," Corey said. "He said he wants to challenge me in a couple of ping-pong games. I believe I'll thrash him too in a short amount of time."

"I don't know… Darren's pretty good at that game. You know, he get his practice in at home because he has one at his place."

"I know. That's where I'm supposed to play him. Maybe you can come witness his defeat, Dad."

"Maybe I will," Calvin said with a smile.

Chapter 14

*I*t was a beautiful, sunny morning as Calvin sat at his desk in his office, gazing out of his large glass window in downtown Southfield, the next day. He couldn't seem to get his mind off of his encounter with Patrice. After a while, he got up and left out of his office, heading to Simon's office. Simon's door was opened slightly when Calvin approached. He knocked on his door and peeked his head in.

"Simon... you have a moment?"

"Calvin, yeah, come in."

Calvin opened the door enough to walk in and he sat down in one of the chairs in front of Simon's desk.

Simon asked, "Is something wrong?"

"No, not at all," Calvin told him. "We're getting ready to develop a couple of business developments in Dallas, right?"

"Yes. As a matter of fact, starting on next Monday."

"Do you already have someone to head up those projects?"

"Well, I've chosen Paul for it because he doesn't have a family and doesn't mind going. I figured you wouldn't want to be away from your family for that long."

"For how long?" asked Calvin.

"Three weeks… possibly more."

"That's not bad. And I've been wanting to see what the Dallas office is like anyway."

"Well, to be honest, Calvin, I would rather you head those projects just because you have a little more experience than Paul. I was just being considerate of your family," Simon explained. "However, I'm fine with it as long as your family is fine with it. You know family comes first with me."

"I'm sure they'll be fine with it."

"Well, you know your family better than I do," said Simon. "Okay. I'll let Paul know that you will be going instead of him, and have Darlene make your travel arrangements. Just let me know if anything changes between now and Monday."

"I will. Thanks, Simon." He stood up and shook Simon's hand.

"Thank you, Calvin." Calvin left Simon's with a smile on his face as he headed back to his office. Back in his office, Calvin finished up some paperwork and cleaned off his desk. He got on his computer and logged into his email account to search for Patrice's company email address. After locating it, he sent her an email: 'Hey Patrice, I'm coming your way to head up those projects I told you about. I'll look for you when I get to the office.' He leaned back into his chair and said to himself, 'I'm going to Dallas,' as he smiled slightly.

After snapping out of his day dream, he got up and walked over to a co-worker's office whose door was half way open. Calvin knocked before entering.

"Hey, Gary… you used to live in Dallas, right?"

"Yeah, about six years ago."

"What's the weather like there during this time?"

"A lot warmer than here. What, are you going there?"

"Yeah, I'll be heading up a couple of new projects there starting on Monday," Calvin told him.

"Oh, nice. How long is the assignment?"

"Three weeks."

"Well, that's plenty of time to take in a few sights. You'll love it there," Gary told him.

"I'm sure I will. Thanks, man."

"No, problem." Calvin returned to his office with nothing but Dallas on his mind. Patrice was mixed up in there as well.

Chapter 15

"**D**avid, why are you eating your food like there's no tomorrow?" Elaina asked as she watched David gobble his food down. It was a little after nine on Saturday morning and Calvin, Elaina, Katrina, Corey and David were all at the kitchen table eating breakfast. Their morning meal consisted of scrambled eggs, country sausage links, toast with butter and grape jelly, and orange juice.

David answered his mom, "Trying to hurry up so Daddy and I can go out to the field today."

"I almost forgot about that, David," Calvin said.

"Are we going?"

"Yeah, we'll go out there for a little bit."

"A little bit? You leave out tomorrow night for three weeks. Can't you spend more than just a little bit with him?" asked Elaina. "There's no one else to help him with football other than just the practice he gets at school."

"I can try," Corey said.

"Thanks, Corey, but it might as well be momma if you gone do it," David said, while everyone snickered except for Elaina.

With an attitude, Elaina said, "Excuse me?"

"Sorry, Momma, but you know you don't know a lot about football."

"You don't know what I know, David. However, I would rather have someone with more experience help you."

David, Corey and Katrina snickered while Calvin just shook his head.

"Well, what about Darren?" Calvin suggested.

"He might be able to, but it's not the same as having his dad do it. Remember? These are things a dad spends time doing with his son," said Elaina.

"Well, we can start back up when I get back from Dallas."

"Oh Dad, who's going to pick me up from the center after school while you're gone?" Corey asked.

"I already talked to Darren, and he said he'll bring you home."

Elaina said to Calvin, "I still don't see why your boss couldn't find someone else to go. I hate inconveniencing people." She was not happy with the news of Calvin having to go to Dallas. Neither were his kids.

"Well, I have more experience than the other guy. So, he chose me to head up the projects."

Katrina asked, "Will you be staying with Uncle Tony, Daddy?"

"No, in a corporate apartment, but I'm sure I'll see him," Calvin told her. "David, I guess we better get out there before it gets too hot."

David quickly got up from the table as he was finished eating his breakfast anyway, and dressed in his gym clothes already. He put his plate in the sink.

Calvin stood up from the table and did the same. Then both of them left the kitchen. Elaina, Corey, and Katrina were still chowing down on their breakfast.

"Momma, Daddy has never had to leave for that long. I'm not cool with that," Katrina said.

Corey nodded in agreement to what Katrina said, while stuffing his mouth.

"Yeah, I know, Trina. Hopefully, it'll go by fast," said Elaina.

Chapter 16

"*C*ome on, David! Keep it high and tight!" Calvin told his son when he threw the football to him at the Southfield Neighborhood Community Center football field. It was somewhat cold on that morning, but the sun was out. Calvin and David was dressed appropriately, although it wouldn't have mattered to David. He was just gung ho about his dad working with him.

Calvin watched David as he ran with the football. He said, "There you go! Let's work on that one more time, David."

David threw the football back to his dad while he trotted back to his original position. He took off running again as Calvin threw the football to him. He caught the football and ran in the opposite direction of Calvin.

"Catch the ball with your hands out in front of you! Don't let it get to your body!" Calvin told him.

David threw the ball back to his dad and then trotted toward him. "So Daddy, what position you played?"

"You'll never guess."

"Well… you don't look like you were fast at all… and you probably weren't tall either. A tight end?"

"Boy, you must be crazy. I was Adrian Peterson before there was an Adrian Peterson. I was a running back like you."

"Oh snap! For real, Pops?"

"Yep."

"That's dope!" David told his dad as he nodded. "I just thought about it… you won't be here for my championship game."

Calvin replied, "Aww man, David. I sure won't." He actually didn't think about that when he opted to take on the projects in Dallas. He said, "I'll try to finish up the projects early so I can get back in time for it."

"I hope so. How long are you gone for again?"

"Three weeks. Speaking of that, we need to go so I can finish packing."

"Yeah, don't remind me," David said under his breath.

Calvin began walking slowly off of the football field toward the Range Rover with David following him.

He turned around to David and said, "You said something, David?"

"I said, yeah, I'm behind you," David said.

"We'll get back on the grind when I return from Dallas."

"Alright."

"And *if* I don't make it back in time for the championship, I know you'll do fine. Just make sure you do what we worked on today," Calvin instructed. "I'm gonna try my best to get back in time, though."

"Yes, sir," David answered his dad with a slight smile as he walked beside him, but in the back of his mind, he wondered if he would really be at his game. "Thanks for helping me today, Daddy," he told Calvin before getting into the SUV. They both got in.

"You got it. And this is just the beginning," Calvin told him. "There's still a lot of work to be put in, David. I haven't seen enough to show me yet you can make it in the pros; let alone, college."

"Well, I just have to show you, Pops!" David said. "That's why I need you there at the game. And I'm still banking on Pastor G putting in a good word for me to the man upstairs."

"If that's what you still wanna do, David, be my guest," Calvin said while shaking his head. He started up his SUV and they left the center.

Chapter 17

"*I* want you all to meditate on the scriptures we discussed tonight for the rest of the week. Are there any prayer requests or testimonies?" Pastor Gillesby asked the small congregation, as he brought bible study to a close on that Wednesday evening of the following week. He quickly scanned the sanctuary to see if any hands would go up. No one raised their hand.

Elaina was one of the few sitting among the small crowd of people, in the third row from the front on the left side of the sanctuary.

"Well alright, I'll see ya back here on Sunday. Be blessed everyone," Pastor Gillesby said before leaving the pulpit.

People began dispersing the sanctuary while Elaina, still seated, searched through her purse for her keys. There were still a limited amount of people standing around chitchatting. A sophisticated and sharp in the way she dressed and in mind, seventy-year-old African-American church mother named Mother Newsome, caught sight of Elaina. Mother Newsome left the church member she was speaking with and walked over to Elaina. Mother Newsome was the kind of church mother who was very in tune to God. She didn't have to know you in order to be able to tell you what was going on in your life. It was like she had a megaphone connected from God's mouth to her ears.

"Elaina, how you doing?"

"Oh, hello Mother Newsome. I've been okay. How've you been?"

"Busy praying… especially for you and your family."

Elaina asked, "You have?"

"Everything alright with Calvin?"

"Yes, as far as I know. He's away on a business trip for a few weeks right now."

"Hmm…"

"Hmm?" Elaina said with curiosity. "Did God show you something, Mother Newsome? Because normally your 'hmm's' mean something is wrong."

"Let's just say I'm glad you showed up tonight," said Mother Newsome. "He needs a change of heart."

With concern, Elaina asked, "Who needs a change of heart?"

"Your husband."

"What do you mean, Mother Newsome?"

"He's carrying a *strong* bitterness in his heart which is going to backfire against him if he doesn't get rid of it. That's what bitterness does, you know. Who is he angry with?"

"How do you even know? Never mind, I forgot who I'm talking to," she said underneath her breath with her head down. She lifted her head and said, "The only person I can think of right now, is his dad; even though what happened to him was well over thirty years ago. He's still angry with him and won't let it go."

"Do you know folks carry around bitterness for that long, and even longer? I remember you told me that his dad was a deacon and had cheated on his mother."

By now, Elaina had given up on trying to locate her keys inside her purse. She knew she was going be there for a little while.

"Yeah, and he said sometimes even a little violent, too," Elaina added. "Calvin was the one who actually caught him at the woman's house. I believe he was about thirteen when that happened."

"My God! And I imagine he's never gotten over that hurt."

"No. He said he'll never forgive him."

"Well, I can understand why he's hurt, but baby, people don't realize the enemy uses unforgiveness as a toy. It's a stronghold. It's a trap. It's poison, you hear me? It's-."

"Bad!" Elaina quickly interrupted. "I get the picture, Mother Newsome. And I've told him that. Well... not like that, but something similar. I just don't know if he listened."

"I sure hope so. It's not good to carry mess like that to your grave. And time is short here on earth. Jesus is coming back soon. Why waste it being bitter and angry with someone?"

"Amen to that," Elaina told Mother Newsome as she looked at the time on her watch. "Just keep for praying us, Mother Newsome. Please keep praying."

"I will, baby. I most certainly will." Mother Newsome gave Elaina a hug.

Elaina said, "I guess we better get out of here before they turn the lights off on us. I don't know about you, Mother Newsome, but I can't see in the dark."

They both chuckled as they got up and left out of the sanctuary.

Chapter 18

*I*t was a little after six on this slightly warm evening in Dallas, Texas. Calvin was chilling back on the sofa after he loosened up his tie and put his keys on the center table. Then, he grabbed the remote sitting by him on the sofa and turned the T.V. on.

Patrice strolled into the living room. She had changed out of her work clothes into something more comfortable, a pair of black leggings with a gray long sleeve mesh tunic that somewhat dropped off the shoulders, and a black tank top under it. She still wanted to look presentable in front of Calvin. Patrice sat on the sofa beside him.

"I'm glad to see you took me up on my offer to stop by," Patrice said.

"Yeah, I have some time to kill before dinner."

"Speaking of eating… you know, I forgot to give you these when you dropped me off at the airport." Patrice laid

Calvin's cuff links on the table beside his keys. She had them in her hand when she came out of her bedroom.

Calvin was surprised, but relieved.

"I've had them in my purse. You left them in the cafeteria last week."

"Thank you. I was wondering what I did with them," Calvin told her as she stood to go into the kitchen. She had a beautiful apartment decorated with classy furniture in warm colors. There were two burnt orange arm chairs made in textured fabric, that faced each other and sat on each side of the sofa. A burnt orange and tan striped sofa also in textured fabric and glass center table, sat in between. On the sofa, were two large tan accent pillows in each corner of the sofa. And on her center table in the middle, sat a beautiful tan oblong shape ceramic vase filled with burnt orange decorative balls with splashes of tan and white on them. Against a wall facing the center table and furniture was a 50" LED T.V. on a small cherry oak stand. And hanging right above the T.V. was a large canvas painting of a white long vase full of assorted white flowers and greenery with a dark gold background. This same painting was also on the wall by her bedroom which led into the living room. All of the walls were painted in taupe and there were dark hard wood floors throughout the apartment. Her kitchen opened out into the living and dining area. The dining area wasn't far from the living room. It was separate; however, still in plain view.

104

The dining set was a round glass tabletop paired with three wide legs that intersect. The base of the table was made of dark wood, and there were four dark gray fabric chairs around it. In the kitchen, there were dark gray, beige and dark brown granite countertops with dark cherry oak cabinetry. The appliances were all stainless steel.

"Yeah, I meant to give them to you, but completely forgot. Sorry about that," she said. She began taking a few things out to cook for dinner. Then asked, "Didn't I tell you the Dallas office was nice?"

"Yeah, you did. This is also a nice place you got here," Calvin said.

"Thank you," she replied. "Can I get you something to drink?"

"What do you have?"

"I have champagne, soda, juice and of course, water."

"I'll take a glass of champagne."

"Coming right up. And you know, you're welcome to stay for dinner if you want."

"I just may do that. Thank you," Calvin said while smiling.

"How long do you have to be here?"

"Supposed to be for three weeks," he answered.

Patrice came out of the kitchen with two glasses filled with champagne and sat down on the sofa, handing one glass to Calvin. "So, your wife was okay with that?"

"She was fine with it. I told her my boss chose me to go. My associate doesn't have the experience I have anyway."

"Impressive, but why do I have a feeling you asked Simon to send you?" she said with a slight a smile.

Suddenly, a knock was heard at the door.

"You expecting company?" asked Calvin.

"No," she replied as she stood up and walked over to the door, looking through the peep hole. "It's Tony!" she murmured. Then yelled, "Just a minute!" She told Calvin, "Go into my room and close the door."

Calvin jumped up from the sofa and rushed into Patrice's bedroom, closing the door behind him. Patrice opened the door and said, "Tony!"

"Surprise!" said Tony.

"Yes, it is!" Patrice told him with a half-smile. "What are you doing here? And I'm sorry, come in."

Tony walked into her apartment, standing by the sofa.

"These are for you." He handed her a dozen of red roses wrapped in white cellophane. "I hope it's okay that I stopped by."

"These are beautiful. Thank you," she told him as she admired and smelled them. "And no, it's fine. I just wasn't expecting you."

"I'm sorry. I just wanted to stop by and say hello. I figured you were settled back in from Southfield by now," said Tony, while surveying her apartment. "You have a really nice apartment, Patrice."

"Thank you, Tony," she replied while attempting to stand in front of her center table to block the glasses filled with champagne, cuff links and keys; however, it didn't work.

"You have company? Or... a boyfriend I don't know about or *should* know about?"

"It's just..." Patrice was stumped and couldn't answer right away, as she observed Tony picking up the cuff links off of the center table and inspecting them. Tony's face was overcome with perplexity.

He looked at every detail on them. Then said, "These look like the cuff links I especially had made for Calvin. How did they get here?"

"Well... I actually saw him when I had my meeting at the office on last Monday."

"Yeah, I remember you said you had to stay over for an unexpected meeting at the office, but you didn't tell me you saw C.J."

"Well, he was nice enough to join me for lunch in the cafeteria so I wouldn't have to eat by myself. He ended up getting ketchup on one of his cuff links and took them off to clean them, but forgot to take them with him when he went

107

back to his office. So, I just put them in my purse so no one would take them," she explained. "I actually forgot I had them until I got back here."

"Oh. Well, I'll call him for you and let him know." Tony quickly pulled out his cell phone and proceeded to call Calvin before Patrice could say anything. She backed away from Tony, turning her back toward him.

Patrice said to herself, "I sure hope his phone is on vibrate."

Tony took his phone away from his ear because he could hear the ringing coming from inside the apartment.

Patrice said to herself, "Shoot."

He walked slowly toward Patrice's bedroom and pushed opened the door. Patrice called out, "Tony!" hoping to stop him, but was unsuccessful.

"C.J.?" said Tony.

Calvin stepped out of Patrice's bedroom. Patrice dropped her head, shaking it.

"What are you doing here?" Tony asked.

"I'm here on a business trip."

"No, not here in Dallas. What are you doing here, at Patrice's? Better yet, does Laina know you're here?"

Calvin was stumped without a response and dropped his head, while Patrice looked away.

"I guess not..." Tony drew back his fist to put a dent into Calvin's face, until Calvin caught his hand and yelled, "T.B. wait! I haven't done anything."

Tony said sternly, "Maybe not by your definition. And if you haven't yet, you're setting yourself up to do something. You need to think about what you're doing, C.J.!"

"But I haven't done anything, T.B.!" Calvin asserted. "Are you gonna tell Laina about this?"

Tony didn't answer right away. He finally said, "I don't know. I may not have to. Things have a way of being exposed, you know."

Patrice stood off to the side silently, still holding on to the roses Tony gave her.

"Man, C.J., I don't get you. You say you don't wanna be like your pops. Well, you sure are starting to follow in his footsteps."

Calvin angrily yelled, "Look! I didn't do what he did!"

"But you're not far from it," Tony said with obvious disgust. He was crushed at seeing his best friend with the woman he was trying to get acquainted with. Tony walked over to Patrice, snatched the roses from her and proceeded to the door. He said, "Bye Patrice." And walked out of the door without looking back, leaving the door open.

Patrice rushed over to the door and yelled, "Tony!" but he ignored her. She went ahead and shut the door.

Calvin retired to the sofa without one word. Patrice walked up to the sofa behind him and laid her hand on his shoulder.

She asked, "You alright, Calvin?"

"Yeah, I'm fine," Calvin said as Patrice walked around to the front of the sofa and sat down beside him.

"I didn't mean to stir up trouble between you guys. I really didn't."

"No, don't worry about it."

"And, I wasn't trying to eavesdrop, but what was Tony talking about when he said you're starting to follow in your pop's footsteps?"

"He said that because I caught my dad cheating on my mom when I was a teenager. T.B. was with me."

"Oh wow. I'm so sorry," she told him. "Well, maybe it is a bad idea for you to be over here, Calvin. I don't want to cause any trouble with you and your wife."

"No, you won't," Calvin reassured her. "Sometimes, Tony gets a little jealous. I don't know why he would be jealous anyway. It's not like you have feelings for me."

"Well now, you are handsome and I do wish you weren't married… but no, there's nothing for him to be jealous about."

"Well, he didn't stay around long enough to see that," Calvin stated. "And you know what… I think I will stay for dinner, if you don't mind. I don't know where all the good food places are yet."

"No, that's totally fine with me. You're welcome to stay. I owe you anyway for taking me to the airport last week."

"Oh, you don't owe me anything… but a nice meal won't hurt."

"You got it." Patrice smiled. She got up from the sofa to go into the kitchen to prepare dinner. Patrice had already taken out enough meat for the two of them, with the assumption he would say yes.

Chapter 19

*I*t was a chilly evening in Southfield, Michigan, but not too chilly for the football fans packed in the stands at Montgomery Rose High School. The stands were filled with shouting fans for both the MRHS Tigers and the Albert E. Graves High School Raptors. The cheerleaders below the crowd on the Tigers side were pumping up the fans with their high energy. They were dressed in all of their glory in the colors of orange, black and white along with the band as they stirred up a movement in some of the fans that dared to believe they had some rhythm. In other words, a few of them couldn't dance and it was evident by their offbeat moves. On the field, football players, coaches and those who assisted with the teams filled the sidelines. A few college football scouts were in the mix as well, but in the stands. There was no mistaking which game you were at as there were banners that lined the metal chain link fences with "VI A Regional Championship."

Among the pumped up crowd was David's fan club which consisted of Elaina, Corey, Katrina, Michelle and Darren. They were all standing, blowing each other's ears out as they cheered for David running with the football. Michelle was Elaina's youngest sister who would sometimes come and support David at his games. The Tigers head coach, Max Stevens, a somewhat tall average looking Caucasian man in his mid-forties, watched with confidence along with his teammates and other coaches as David neared the goal line.

Elaina yelled, "Go David! Go!"

While Corey yelled, "You got it, Bro!"

Then Darren yelled, "Let's go, David!"

David crossed the goal line for a touchdown as anticipated and did a quick celebration with a few teammates while in the end zone.

Elaina announced to the crowd sitting around her, "That's my baby!"

Some clapped and some looked at her like she was crazy. She quickly sat down.

Then Michelle announced to the crowd like her sister did, "And that's my nephew!"

Again, some laughed and some looked at her as if she was crazy also, but Michelle could care less. She continued to stand and clap for her nephew.

David ran over to the sideline as he was congratulated by the coaches and other teammates. He looked over to where his fan club was sitting with excitement on his face initially, until he only took notice of his mom, sister, brother, aunt and uncle sitting there. Elaina gave him a thumbs up when she caught his eye. David returned a thumbs up back at her with a half-smile, and turned around to put his focus back on the game.

Meanwhile in Dallas, Patrice and Calvin were sitting at her dining table, enjoying a delectable meal she had cooked for them: chicken breast with gravy, mashed potatoes and French style green beans. And alongside each of their plates stood a glass of champagne. The lighting in the room was normal and the T.V. was still on, but the volume was really low. It really was just a casual dinner they were having.

"This is really good, Patrice. I'm glad I stayed."

"Thank you. There's more if you want it."

"No, this is perfect," Calvin said.

"You told me a little bit about your dad… what about your mom? Are they still together?"

"Well, my mom passed away a few years ago, and I don't talk to my dad. I haven't talked to him in years," Calvin told her.

"I'm sorry to hear about your mom." She took a sip of her champagne. "And that's too bad about your dad, too. Do you have any siblings?"

"No, just me."

"Gotcha. And I see you made sure that wasn't repeated with your own family."

Calvin smiled and nodded. He said, "Oh, you're talking about Trina, Corey and David."

"Yes. They seem to be great kids."

"They are," said Calvin. "I know one of them though, is angry with me right now because I'm missing his game. I told him I would try to get back for it, but it just didn't work out. I know I'll hear about it when I get back."

Back at the game, the scoreboard showed the time counting down with only thirty seconds left on the clock. The opposing team had thirty-three points while the Tigers had twenty-seven. The center hiked the football off to the quarterback and he handed the football off to David at the twenty-yard line. Nearly everyone on each side of the field was standing up cheering and sweating bullets as the clock counted down to zero. David, once again, was reaching for a touchdown. This one was really important. His fan club was cheering him on to help push him over the goal line.

Elaina yelled, "Come on, David!"

Katrina screamed, "Go, David!"

And Michelle yelled, "Go boy!"

115

And it seemed like Darren would always give that last hurrah. He yelled, "You're almost there!"

David's quick speed and agility aided him in crossing the goal line with only five seconds left on the clock. He threw the football down in the end zone as his teammates rushed over to pick him up. The clock was now at zero. The Tigers fans, along with David's fan club, were clapping for him as he rode on the shoulders of his teammates. David took one last observation of his fan club to see if one more person had been added to the bunch. When he saw that it was the same, David sucked his teeth and shook his head as his teammates lowered him from their shoulders. The rest of his team and coaches continued to congratulate him on a job well done.

Chapter 20

*A*t the kitchen table, Elaina relaxed with a hot cup of lemon and honey tea to soothe her voice from all of the shouting she did at the game, as she reflected upon how well her son did. She had a smile of gratitude on her face as she stared at her cup.

She said, "Thank you Lord, for what you did tonight with David." Then took her cell phone out and dialed Calvin.

Calvin answered, "Laina?"

"Hey. The Tigers won the championship! They're going to State!"

"Wow, really?"

"They did. And your son had a lot to do with it. He actually scored the winning touchdown."

"That's good to hear! Where is he now?" Calvin asked. He was hoping to talk with David to smooth things over before he got back home.

"When David got home, he ate, took a bath and went straight to bed," Elaina told him. "Oh, and your favorite person came to the game to see David play."

"Who's my favorite person?"

"Now, you should know Michelle is. Darren came, too."

"Your sister came to the game? And I bet she talked bad about me for not being there, didn't she?"

"Well, you know how that goes. It wouldn't be Michelle if she didn't. You should know that by now," Elaina said as she took her empty cup over to the sink. "David was really disappointed that you weren't able to make it." She stood leaning back on the counter waiting to hear his response.

"Yeah, I'm sure he was. I wasn't able to leave out early like I was hoping to. I really was trying to get this pre-planning done and over with this week, but it's taking longer than I expected."

"You're not going to have to stay longer, are you?"

"No, I'll be home at the end of next week. I was just trying to shorten my time here to two weeks instead of three."

"Okay good, because I invited my dad, mom and Michelle over for dinner in two weeks."

Calvin replied, "That's fine. I'll be home in time."

"Okay. So, how's it going there?" Elaina asked.

"It's going good. Dallas is really nice, *and* huge."

"Have you seen Tony yet?"

"Yeah, I did. We talked some, but haven't had a chance to hang out yet."

"Well... hopefully you will before you leave there," she said before sitting back down in her chair at the kitchen table. "Well, babe, I'm beat. I just wanted to tell you about David's game. Maybe David will give you a call tomorrow and tell you about it. I don't know... he may not ever wanna talk to you," said Elaina, with a smirk on her face.

"You may be right, Laina. Well, tell David I'm proud of him. And tell Corey and Trina I said hey."

"I will. I love you."

"Love you, too," Calvin replied.

Elaina hung up with Calvin as she arose from the kitchen table. She turned off the light and retired to her bed.

Chapter 21

"**E**verything okay, Calvin?" Patrice asked, as she approached the sofa where he was sitting. He had put his cell phone on Patrice's center table after just speaking with Elaina.

"Yeah, everything's good. My son won their championship game."

"Really? That's wonderful!" she told Calvin as she sat down beside him on the sofa.

Calvin said, "Yeah, it is." Then smiled slightly. "Hey, thank you for dinner. It was really good."

"Oh, you're welcome. You know… there's this nice restaurant I would love to take you to at the end of the week, if you wanna go. It's actually not far from the office, and they have great food."

"Yeah, sure. That sounds good," replied Calvin. "Well, guess I better get out of here. I have an early morning." He grabbed his keys, cuff links and cell phone off of the center table, putting them in his pocket. He stood up and walked over to the door. Patrice followed him to see him out. "Thanks again for dinner," he said.

Patrice said, "No problem. I'll see you tomorrow." She opened the door and snuck in a kiss on Calvin's lips as he began walking out of the door.

Calvin was without words.

"I'm sorry. I shouldn't have done that," she said, acting like she was embarrassed by her actions. "I guess I just really enjoyed your company this evening. It's been a long time since I've had that."

"I... better go before I find myself doing something I shouldn't. See you tomorrow... at the office." He quickly exited her apartment.

Patrice shut the door behind him, then stood there leaning back on the door wearing a slight smile on her face. A feeling of butterflies overcame her stomach as the gratification of placing her lips upon Calvin's lips sunk in.

On the other side of the door, Calvin stood at the elevator for a few moments as he tried to wrap his brain around what had just taken place. He shook his head as if to dismiss his thoughts, then stepped inside of the elevator when it opened. Once inside, he pressed one and leaned back against the wall of the elevator. A slight smile came upon his face as he again shook his head, and thought to himself, "I still got it."

Chapter 22

*A*t the Main Street Bistro, just about every table was filled that evening with talkative folks stuffing their mouths with tasty food items from the menu. There was a divine aroma outside and throughout the restaurant of both classic American and French cuisines. It was a popular eclectic restaurant that had been around for many years, and was seated right in the heart of Downtown Dallas. There was never really any downtime for their chefs, hosts or hostesses. They were always busy with new comers and old comers. If they were not there just to consume their delicious food, it was for the great atmosphere and exquisite wine collection. And their prices were not all that bad either.

In the midst of this busy bistro, was a table seated at the front of the restaurant with three African-American hairstylists enjoying each other's company while they gossiped and put away food and wine.

April was chowing down on a delicious looking cobb salad, Dana had filet mignon with a loaded baked potato, and Michelle was devouring a roasted chicken and garlic potatoes dish.

April asked Michelle, "Did you all see what Benita had on today?"

"Yes girl, I did," responded Michelle while stuffing her mouth with chicken. She said, "Who wears that to a hair show?"

"Right!" April said.

"But her hair was cute, though," Michelle told them.

April replied, "Yeah, it was. I can't argue with that," as she took a sip of her Chardonnay. She said, "I absolutely *love* when we get together for these shows… gives us a chance to catch up and most of all eat some great food."

"Yes!" Dana asserted while nodding. She inserted a fork full of her loaded baked potato into her mouth.

As April scanned the room, she noticed one of her clients a few tables away near the back wall of the restaurant.

"Oh wow, there's my client," April told her friends. With Dana sitting right across from April, she took a quick look over at the table April was talking about before putting the next bite in her mouth. April said, "Michelle, you did her hair for me a few weeks ago."

"Oh, Patrice?" Michelle asked as she was still stuffing her face, not trying to look at anybody but her plate.

April said, "Yeah. And that man she's with is…"

Michelle quickly turned around to lay eyes on him herself. Her food was important, but so was a man. She exclaimed, "Calvin! My brother-in-law!"

April said quietly, "Hot." Then said, "Oh!" She was astonished as things quickly came together in her head. Then murmured, "Oh… Not good…."

Michelle didn't waste a second pulling out her cell phone. "I'm calling my sister."

April and Dana watched her with suspense as she dialed her sister using FaceTime.

After a couple of rings, Elaina's face appeared on Michelle's phone. "Laina, hey."

"Hey. To what do I owe a FaceTime call from you?" asked Elaina. "And where are you?"

"I'm at a restaurant in Dallas eating with a couple of friends."

"Oh, what are you doing in Dallas?"

Michelle responded, "I came for a hair show."

"You know… Calvin is there, too, working on a project."

"Well, not right now he's not," Michelle informed her. "Right now, he's here at the restaurant with this person…" She flipped the phone around and pointed it toward Calvin's table.

"That's Patrice!" Elaina exclaimed.

Michelle flipped her phone back around to her. "You know her?"

"Yeah. I met her when she and Tony came to Calvin's company fall festival. She works for the same company Calvin does," Elaina responded with bewilderment.

"You talking about Calvin's friend, Tony?"

"Yeah. Tony and Calvin met her at Jay's Lounge."

Michelle said, "She came to the salon to get her hair done some weeks ago. She's a client of my friend, April. I should've known she was trouble then."

April shrugged her shoulders at Michelle. She whispered, "Sorry."

"You want me to take the phone over there?" Michelle asked.

"No, Michelle. I'll handle it. I'll talk to you later."

Michelle replied, "Alright." She hung up with her sister and continued eating.

"Michelle, I am so sorry. I didn't know," April told her.

"No girl, he's the one who's gone be sorry," Michelle said as she sipped on her wine.

April asked, "Are you going to let him know you're here?"

"No, but if I didn't have to leave out late tonight, I sure would follow his behind."

"Knowing you, yeah, you would. Wouldn't she, Dana?" April asked.

"Yep," replied Dana.

"Whatever," Michelle said with a slight smirk. "I know one thing... he's got some explaining to do to my sister."

Chapter 23

"*M*omma, was that Aunt Michelle?" David asked as he walked into the kitchen. He could hear her voice as he approached the kitchen.

Elaina was at the kitchen table staring at the wall with watery eyes. Her cell phone was on the table. She tried to quickly wipe her eyes before David saw her.

David walked up to his mom and took a closer look at her face. "Momma, what's wrong?"

"Yes, that was her. She just saw your dad at a restaurant with another woman." Elaina went ahead and told him because she figured her kids would find out sooner or later. She never sugar coated anything with her kids when they became a certain age. She believed they were mature enough to hear whatever she had to say. She always told them, "I'd rather you hear it from me than out there on the

127

streets." Perhaps that way of thinking came from her many years of teaching.

David asked, "In Dallas?"

"Yes, son. All the way in Dallas." She told him as she continued to stare at the wall.

"Did you talk to him yet? Maybe she thought it was him and it really wasn't."

Elaina said, "It was him, David." She got up from the table as she grabbed her cell phone. Anger began to rise up in David which Elaina could see. She said, "You don't have to worry about it, son. I'll handle it. Alright?"

David nodded. Elaina exited the kitchen and headed to her bedroom, while David left out of the kitchen on the way to the family room where his brother and sister were. Cory was sitting in a chair reading a book while Katrina was on the sofa watching T.V.

"Man, y'all, Aunt Michelle just saw Daddy with another lady at a restaurant in Dallas," David told Corey and Katrina.

Corey pulled his book down from in front of his face. Katrina grabbed the remote and placed the T.V. on mute.

"For real? How do you know?" Katrina asked.

"Momma just told me. That was Aunt Michelle on the phone."

"Why would he do that? He's supposed to be there working," Katrina stated.

Corey asked, "Did she call to ask him about it yet?"

"I don't think so."

"Well, he sure can't call anybody a hypocrite," Corey said.

Then Katrina asked, "Did Momma say who the lady was?"

"No. But he's gone pay if he's cheating on my momma," answered David.

"What are you going to do, David?" Corey wondered.

"I don't know. I'm already mad at him for missing my game. This just makes me even more madder."

"You mean even madder?" said Corey. His ears never missed an opportunity to correct someone's grammar.

"Whatever, Corey. Sorry I'm not as smart as you," David replied.

Katrina said, "Well, I'm gonna ask Momma and find out who she was."

"Maybe we should call Grandma and Grandpa James, or Uncle Darren?" suggested David.

But Katrina responded, "They don't need to know. That's just gonna get Daddy into more trouble."

"I agree," said Corey. "We definitely can't tell Grandma and Grandpa James. Grandpa James would have Dad's head on a platter. And Uncle Darren will probably find out about it eventually anyway."

129

"I hope Aunt Michelle got on him," Katrina said.

"That's really bad news that she saw him. Dad will never live this down as long as she's around," Corey stated. Although somewhat mad, David managed to break out in a little laugh. "What are you laughing at?" Corey asked.

"You just did a rhyme."

Katrina sighed and rolled her eyes at David, while Corey just stared at him with an annoyed look on his face.

While the in depth conversation was going on in the family room, Elaina sat at the foot of her bed with her cell phone in her hand as she stared at herself in the mirror on her dresser.

She said, "Okay Lord, I'm going to give him a chance to explain himself. It could've been a business meeting and he just forgot to tell me. We'll see. You know… it would've been nice if you had given Mother Newsome this specific detail to tell me." She dialed Calvin.

He was at his corporate apartment dressed in jogging pants and a T-shirt, sitting on the sofa watching T.V. He picked up his cell phone when he heard it ring and saw that it was Elaina calling. He answered it.

"Laina?"

"Hey."

He asked, "What's going on?"

"Nothing. Just calling to see how things are going there," Elaina told him.

"It's going good. Just trying to wrap things up before I come home."

"Yeah, I'm ready for you to come home. So, what have you been eating since you don't cook?"

"I know how to cook some things, but I've been eating out mostly."

"That's what I figured. You eat out this evening or cooked whatever those some things are?"

"I went to this nice bistro place this evening."

Elaina nodded as she smiled slightly, in anticipation of Calvin telling her about having a meeting there with Patrice. "They have really good food there," he said.

"Oh, really? How did you find it?"

"An associate actually told me about it. I just got something quick and left," Calvin told her.

Elaina went silent for a moment, and shook her head. "Laina."

"Yeah, I'm here," she responded, still out of sorts. "Well, when you see T.B. again, tell him I said hello. I hope and Patrice are hitting it off well. She's at the Dallas office, right?"

"Yeah, she is. But I haven't really seen her. That office is so big."

Anger began to build up silently in Elaina, but her inner strength was holding her back from saying anything yet for some reason.

"Well, if you see her, tell her I said hello also."

"I will."

"Love you, Calvin," she told him, despite being deeply hurt at that moment.

"Love you, too, Laina. See you soon."

Elaina ended the call with her husband and put her cell phone down on the bed. She just sat there on her bed in silence.

"Okay, God, now what? You said you work all things out for our good. How are you going to work this one out? Sometimes you're loud and clear... this time, you're quiet," she told God. "I don't even know what to pray right now. I'm so angry with him," she said to herself. "Convict him... please convict him! Help him to see what he's doing is wrong. It's wrong! Lord, just hurry and bring him back home where he needs to be," prayed Elaina with tears in her eyes.

Chapter 24

Corey and Darren both sweating a little, came back into Darren's house from off of his patio where they had just finished playing a few games of ping-pong. Darren brought him over to play a couple of days after Elaina's ordeal with Calvin. Darren was unaware of what happened and Corey wasn't about to tell him.

Darren's home was located about five miles away from the center in a pretty nice neighborhood in Southfield. It was decorated rather pleasantly for it to be a bachelor pad and kept neat and simple. He had a dark brown leather loveseat that sat on the right side of a matching recliner sofa which surrounded a dark wooden center table. On the table were a few magazines: Jet and Sports Illustrated. There was a navy blue throw blanket that laid on the top of the loveseat. One end table with a lamp sat on the left side of the sofa, and another one on the right between the sofa and loveseat. The lamps had a brown ceramic base with off white burlap shades. The end tables matched the center table. On the wall facing the sofa and loveseat was a mounted 60" flat screen T.V. right above the fireplace. And on a side wall, hung a picture of his mom and one of his grandparents. Corey, David and Katrina really adored Darren and considered him to be a true uncle even though he wasn't biologically. But he'd been a part of their lives since they were born.

Corey walked over to Darren's sofa and plopped down on it by his book bag. Darren went into the kitchen which was near his living room. The kitchen was somewhat spacious and had all oak wood cabinetry. The countertops were laminate in a black, brown and white speckled pattern. A microwave and bread case sat on a counter together while an electric can opener and knife set, sat on another. Right beside the kitchen window stood a rectangular cherry oak table with four matching cushioned chairs.

"Well, I guess they're right about you at the center. You are the ping-pong king," Darren told him while washing his hands.

Corey said, "You better recognize, Uncle Darren!"

Darren laughed. He asked Corey, "You want something to drink?"

"Yes. Some ice cold water would be nice, please."

"You got it." While getting Corey's water, he asked, "So, your dad comes home next week, right?" He walked over to the sofa where Corey was sitting, with a glass of ice water in his hand and sat down close beside Corey while handing the glass to him.

"Yep. I can't wait for him to come home," Corey answered while taking a few sips of his water. Then, he looked at Darren with a mystified expression before the thought of his dad came to mind. "I miss him," Corey said.

Darren placed his hand on Corey's leg. "I'm sure you do, Corey. I kind of fill in as a dad for some of the guys at the center who dads are not around."

"Well, that's cool," Corey told him while continuing to look at Darren sideways. "Uncle Darren, you do know there's plenty of room on this sofa? So you don't have to sit right up under me."

"My bad, Corey. I guess I just wanna make sure you know I'm here for you, you know... with your dad being gone and all." Darren took his hand off of Corcy's leg and scooted over from him.

"Okay. Yeah, literally, you're showing me," Corey said, before jumping up off of the sofa still holding his glass of water. He walked into the kitchen and murmured to himself, "Well, that was weird."

"You have any homework you need my help with? Or you finished at the center?" Darren asked from the sofa.

"No. All done. I'm hungry, though. What do you have in here to eat, Uncle Darren?" Corey put his glass of water down on the counter and began looking in cabinets and in the fridge.

Darren got up from the sofa and joined Corey in the kitchen.

"I'll fix you a sandwich," Darren told him as he laid his hands on Corey's shoulders from behind. Then said, "Some of the guys come here hungry all the time, looking for something to eat."

Corey grabbed his water and quickly walked away from Darren and stood outside of the kitchen. "You're real touchy today, Uncle Darren," said Corey. He began to feel uncomfortable, but just thought he was genuinely being caring because his dad was gone.

"I'm sorry, Corey. I'm just glad I get to spend some time with my nephew," Darren said, then opened the fridge taking out deli meat and condiments. He grabbed the white loaf of bread sitting on the counter and began fixing Corey a sandwich.

Corey sat down at the kitchen table. "So, what other guys from the center come here?"

"Let's see… mostly Kenny, DeWayne and Avery. They're the ones I normally take to NBA and NFL games when I get tickets," Darren told Corey as he brought out a small plate with a turkey and ham sandwich on it. He placed it in front of Corey on the table alongside his glass of water. "Here you go, man."

"Thanks," said Corey.

Darren sat at the other end of the table as Corey began eating his sandwich. "I plan on getting you and David some NFL tickets. Hopefully, next week."

Corey replied, "David is going to love that."

"Yeah, I know. I actually have a pro football card collection I bet he would like too. I'll show you when you're done eating."

"Yeah, I would like to take a look at it. David can come see it when football season is over. I'll tell him about it though," Corey said as he put away his sandwich. "I'm almost done."

"Okay. Then I'll take you home afterwards."

Corey took one last huge bite of what used to be a sandwich, leaving only a little piece of crust from the bread on his plate. He brushed his hands together, removing any crumbs, and took one last sip of his water to wash the rest down. "Alright, Uncle Darren, where is it?"

"Oh, in my room. I keep it out of sight just in case any sticky fingers come in here. That collection cost me a pretty penny."

Darren and Corey stood up from the table. Darren said, "Come on, I'll show you."

Corey followed Darren to his bedroom. Darren walked to his closest, opened the door and pulled down a box containing the pro football collection while Corey waited patiently by his bed. "Here it is." Darren spread the cards out on his bed so Corey could view them.

Even though Corey always had his head in books all of the time, he was still familiar with football players from watching NFL games on T.V. and playing Madden NFL.

While Corey was intrigued by the card collection, Darren quietly began taking off his belt and undoing his pants while standing behind Corey.

"Wow, this is pretty cool, Uncle Darren!" Corey said as he looked up from the cards and then behind him.

Darren placed his hands on Corey's shoulders again as Corey looked down at Darren's pants. They weren't down *yet,* but unzipped.

Corey asked frantically, "What are you doing, Uncle Darren?"

Chapter 25

"*H*ey, make sure you tell David I'll have those NFL tickets next week for you two," Darren told Corey, as he got out of the passenger front seat of Darren's Dodge pick-up truck after pulling up in front of Corey's house.

Corey grabbed his book bag and slammed Darren's door. He angrily responded, "Yeah, okay." and began walking toward the front door.

"See you later, Corey," said Darren.

Corey continued walking toward the door without another word to Darren. Darren finally drove off. Corey unlocked the front door with his key and walked in.

"Hey, Corey," Elaina said while folding clothes on the sofa in the family room. David was sitting on the floor leaning against the sofa doing his homework.

"Hey," he responded quietly while rushing to his bedroom.

"What's wrong with him?" David asked.

"I'm not sure. Let me go find out." Elaina finished folding the shirt in her hand, then walked to Corey's bedroom. His door was closed. She knocked once, to give him a warning that she was coming in, and opened the door.

Corey always kept a clean room, unlike his brother. He had two chemistry projects he made sitting on his five drawer chest, a volcano and a solar system model. And on his dresser, sat a couple of cologne bottles and two books, one was Ben Carson's 'Think Big' and the Bible. In a corner, he had a dark blue bean bag he'd had for a few years. Sometimes he sat on it while reading. In between his bean bag and chest, sat a small wooden desk and study light on it.

Elaina didn't go all the way inside of his room, but just stood in the doorway. Corey was just sitting on his bed.

She asked, "Corey? You wanna talk about it?"

"No."

"Are you sure? Because obviously, there's something wrong. You never come in like that."

Corey was silent for a moment and then asked, "Did Dad really have to go on that trip?"

"Well yes, I guess so. I would rather he didn't, but I don't think we had a choice in it."

Corey replied, "I wish his boss would have sent somebody else."

"I know," said Elaina. "Is that what you're mad about?"

"No. I just wish Dad was here."

"Yeah, I know, Corey. Are you sure you don't wanna talk?"

"I'm sure," he told his mom.

"Okay. Well, you know where to find me when you're ready."

"I'll be fine. You have enough to worry about with Dad being gone."

"Yeah, I do, Corey. But whatever is bothering you, is important to me."

"It's nothing I can't handle," Corey told his mom, trying to be strong.

Elaina said, "Alright, if you say so, son." She walked over to Corey and kissed him on the forehead before leaving out of his bedroom. She closed his door behind her and went back to the sofa to finish folding clothes.

Corey got up and locked his door.

"What's wrong with him, Momma?" asked David.

"I don't know. Something is wrong, but he won't talk. Maybe he'll tell you."

"I'll find out."

"Well, if you do, let me know."

"Okay," said David.

In his bedroom, Corey sat on the floor beside his book bag in front of his bed with tears streaming down his face.

"God, am I being punished for something I did? What did I do wrong?" asked Corey. "He's supposed to be family! What kind of family does that?" Corey quickly wiped his face when he heard a knock at his door. "Yeah, who is it?"

"Me," answered David.

"What'd you want, David?"

David turned the knob on Corey's door, but found that it was locked. "Open the door and see."

Corey unlocked his door and opened it for David. David walked in and closed the door behind him. Corey sat on his bed while David stood by Corey's dresser.

"Who were you talking to?"

"What, you were listening?" asked Corey.

"I wasn't listening. It's just that my ear caught what you were saying when I came to your door," David explained. He asked, "Bruh, what's going on with you?"

"I can't say."

"Why not?"

"I just can't, David."

"But we talk about everything," David said.

"Yeah, I know. This time, it's not that easy," Corey told him and then dropped his head. "Don't you miss Dad?"

"Yeah, but I'm not a big fan of his right now," David told him while picking up his Polo cologne bottle and smelling it.

"Yeah, I know. I still hate not having him here," said Corey. "If he was here, Uncle Darren wouldn't have to bring me home."

David placed his Polo cologne back on his dresser. "That's what you've been mad about, bruh?"

"Yeah, kind of," said Corey. Then, he said quietly, "Uncle Darren messed with me."

David asked, "He tricked you?" as he walked over to Corey's bean bag and plopped down on it, leaning back.

"No. He messed with me, David… like a guy would mess with a girl."

David said aloud, "Stop lying, Corey!"

"Shh… I'm not."

"You talking about Un-cle Darren?" David wanted to make sure he was hearing right.

"Yes!"

David sat up straight and shouted, "Uncle Darren?" It finally registered with David what his brother was telling him.

"Shh. Yeah, him. I don't want Mom to know."

"Why not, Corey?"

"Because they grew up together and she calls him her brother. I can't tell her!"

143

"So, Corey!" David said and stood up. "Right now, I feel like I'm the smarter one in here."

"But he's getting us NFL tickets next week if I don't say anything."

"I don't care about that, bruh! I mean I do, but... I'm telling Momma." David darted out of Corey's bedroom, heading into the kitchen before Corey could stop him.

Corey yelled, "David!"

David entered the kitchen eager to tell his mom what Corey said. She was at the sink washing dishes while dinner was cooking.

"Momma, I found out what's wrong with Corey."

Elaina stopped washing dishes and turned around to David. "Well, what is it?"

"Just stay calm when I tell you."

"David, what is it?" Elaina was antsy to find out what was bothering her son.

"Corey said Uncle Darren messed with him."

She asked, "Messed with him how?"

"Like how a guy messes with a girl."

Elaina stood silently for a moment. Then, she walked over to the entrance of the kitchen and took a look outside of the kitchen to the right, and to the left. She said, "Are you all setting me up to be punked or something? Because this is *not* funny at all, David!"

144

"No, I'm not, Momma," he told her with a serious face.

Elaina walked back over to the sink and stood against the counter. She yelled, "Corey!"

Corey knew his mom would be calling him shortly.

He shouted, "Ma'am?" from his bedroom door.

She yelled back, "Come here!" Elaina stood in the kitchen with her arms folded, staring at David until Corey came in there. She still was uncertain if she could believe what David had told her.

Corey stood by the kitchen table. With her arms still folded, she asked, "Did Darren do something to you, Corey?"

"I really don't want to say," responded Corey as he looked at his brother.

David looked down as to not make eye contact with him.

"Corey, if he touched you in the wrong way, I need to know. Did he?"

There was a moment of silence before he answered. "Yes," he replied as he held his head down. He didn't want his mom to know because of Darren's status in the family, but more so because he was embarrassed.

Elaina asked angrily, "What did he do?"

"He asked if I wanted to see his pro football card collection after I ate my sandwich. I told him yes. He said it

145

was in his bedroom. So, I followed him in there and waited by his bed while he took it down from his closet and put them out on his bed. While I was looking at them, he came up behind me and started undoing his pants. Then he… you know…"

"No, I don't know. I need to hear it from you."

With his head down, he told her, "He groped me."

Elaina yelled, "He did what?"

David's eyes got big when his brother said, 'He groped me.' That was the first time he had heard that part.

Elaina looked up at the ceiling for a few seconds and sighed, as a means of calming herself down. David and Corey watched her with apprehension.

She said calmly, "David, go ahead and eat. Your sister should be coming in shortly." Then to Corey, she said, "Grab a jacket and let's go."

Corey quickly left out of the kitchen to get a jacket, while his mom grabbed her jacket, purse and keys. Then she and Corey left through the front door.

David stood there in the kitchen frozen, wondering if he should have said anything now.

Chapter 26

*N*eighbors began crowding outside under the street lights and peeping out of their windows as they witnessed flashing blue lights with the sound of sirens, pulling up in front of a neighbor's home. There were two police vehicles. One vehicle had two officers in it and the other had one. The sirens suddenly went silent as the officers shut their vehicles off. A third vehicle pulled up behind the officer vehicles.

It was Elaina and Corey in her gray 2013 S class Mercedes. As the officers stepped out of their vehicles, Elaina and Corey got out of their vehicle as well. They closed the doors and Elaina walked over to the passenger side where Corey was and put her arm around his shoulders as they observed the officers walking up to Darren's front door. It was a tall, somewhat slim Caucasian female officer in her mid-thirties, an average height, but buffed Caucasian male in his early to mid-forties and a tall, buffed African-American male in his late thirties.

The Caucasian male officer knocked. It was a few moments before Darren opened the door. The officer introduced himself while the other two stood behind him with their hands on their weapons, just in case there would be any trouble. And then, the Caucasian male officer told Darren to step outside.

The officer explained why they were there and pointed toward Corey and Elaina. Darren looked over that way.

Elaina had nothing but pure anger written all over her face as she pulled Corey closer to her with the arm she had around his shoulders. Corey, filled with hurt and embarrassment, couldn't even look at him. He dropped his head down.

The crowd outside began to grow as the neighbors who were just peeping out of their windows, made their way out onto their lawns.

The officer read Darren his rights as he took out his handcuffs. He had Darren to turn around and then he cuffed him. He pulled Darren to the side to speak with him further and then told the other two officers to go inside of Darren's home to do a search. Darren didn't hold back on giving any information. It was almost like he was ready to be caught.

Elaina, Corey and Darren's neighbors continued to watch the officers at work. Inside of Darren's home, was a second bedroom where he always kept the door shut. The two officers opened the door revealing a tripod with a camera on it sitting in the middle of the floor in front of a bed, and one dresser with nothing on it. The female officer checked the drawers of the dresser and removed the camera from the tripod. Her partner opened the closet door finding four heavy duty storage boxes. After the female officer couldn't find anything in the dresser drawers, she helped her partner remove the boxes from the closet. They sat them on the bed and looked inside of them. Inside each box were photos of half-dressed boys, mainly African-American, ranging, in what looked like, from ages thirteen to fifteen. The officers placed the tops back onto the boxes and carried them out of the house.

As they placed the boxes in the back seat of the second police vehicle, Elaina removed her arm from around Corey and called the female officer over to her. As Elaina spoke with her, Elaina covered her mouth in disbelief at what she had just been told. The officer that was holding Darren off to the side, walked him to the first police vehicle. As he got ready to get into the back seat of the police vehicle, Elaina's eyes filled with water as she stood there with her hand still over her mouth.

149

Corey, with a solemn face, along with the neighbors watched him get inside the car. The female officer stood on the driver's side of the second police vehicle, while her partner locked the door of Darren's home. He came around to the passenger side of that vehicle, and he and the female officer got inside.

The officer of the first police vehicle came over to Elaina and handed her a card. She was still speechless, but just nodded at the officer. He walked off from her and got in on the driver side of the first police vehicle. Then both police vehicles pulled off.

Elaina stood there with Corey with her arms wrapped around him for a few moments. They both got in the car and left the place that would forever be a horrible memory for both of them.

Chapter 27

"**M**omma, everything alright?" asked Katrina, very concerned as her mom and brother walked into the house after leaving Darren's.

David sat on the floor in front of the sofa while his sister sat on the sofa. They both were watching T.V., waiting for Elaina and Corey to come home. Katrina put the T.V. on mute. Elaina slowly sat down on the sofa alongside Katrina. Corey sat down in the chair nearby.

"Right now... I can't even answer that, Trina," replied Elaina, as she looked at a family photo sitting on an end table. It was like she was in a daze. She said, "I need to call your dad to let him know what's going on." She got up from the sofa to head into the kitchen, but stopped in front of Corey and told him, "Corey... You listen to me. You did nothing wrong. You hear me?"

Corey nodded.

"As a matter of fact, you've helped the other guys he's been doing this to. I feel so stupid because I had no clue. It's sickening just thinking about it."

"You mind if I go to my room now, Mom?" asked Corey.

"That's fine," she told him as he stood up. "Wait… you're not hungry? You didn't eat yet."

"No, I'm not hungry."

"Well, okay." She laid her hand on his shoulder as she faced him. "I'll check in on you in a moment."

"Alright," he replied, and he walked out of the family room, leaving his brother and sister in there. Concern for their brother showed on their faces.

"Alright. You two need to get to bed also. You still have school tomorrow," Elaina told David and Katrina.

"Alright," David said.

"Yes ma'am," replied Katrina.

David stood up from the floor and Katrina from the sofa. Katrina went ahead and left to go to her bedroom.

"Momma, you know this is all Daddy's fault," David told his mom.

"Why you say that, David?"

He answered, "Because if he was here, none of this would've happened." Then he left out of the family room also.

Elaina couldn't say anything, because she knew her son was telling the truth. She went into the kitchen and sat down at the table. She began to shed some tears. She managed to pull herself together before calling Calvin.

He was at his corporate apartment lying in bed with no shirt on and pajama pants, covered by a sheet and comforter. The lights were off. When he heard his cell phone ring, he reached over to turn on the lamp sitting beside him on a night stand. He sat up on the side of the bed to look at his cell phone which was lying on the table as well, and quickly answered it.

"Hey."

"Calvin. Were you sleep yet?" Elaina asked.

"No, not quite. What's up?"

"I'm calling to let you know what happened today with Corey."

"What happened to Corey?" asked Calvin with full attention to whatever she was getting ready to tell him. He was no longer quite sleepy.

"I hadn't had the chance to call you earlier, but Darren... touched Corey in a way he shouldn't have."

"What do you mean in a way he shouldn't have? He hit him?"

"No. Darren touched Corey's private property; you know property that should stay hidden until he's married to a female."

"No. What?" He shook his head. He said, "Darren, seriously? I don't believe that."

"I didn't either, Calvin, but it's true. And come to find out, he had been doing this to other boys."

He stood up and said, "That's crazy, Laina!" He walked around in the bedroom. "Where is Darren now?"

"I had his butt arrested at his home. I didn't know what else to do."

"No, you did right," he assured her. "It might be best that I wasn't there because I would've been joining him in jail. How's Corey?"

"He's okay, but hurt, as you can imagine. I mean... he was Uncle Darren!"

"Yeah, I know. Well, I'm not here much longer. I'm home at the end of next week. I'll call and check in on Corey tomorrow, and see what's going on with Darren when I get back."

"Okay. And yeah, I'm sure Corey will wanna talk to you. It was hard for him to talk to me about it."

"I'll call and talk to him," said Calvin.

"Alright. Love you."

"Love you, too," Calvin told Elaina, and then hung up. He wandered around in his bedroom with his hands interlocked behind his head for a few moments, before he sat back down on the side of the bed and raised his head toward the ceiling. "God... I'm really not good at this praying thing.

Never have been... but... I know this is all my fault. Corey's a good kid and didn't deserve this." He stared at the wall in front of him. He said to himself, "What am I doing here? Maybe Laina was right." He raised his head back up to the ceiling and said, "Whatever it takes God... I'll do it."

Chapter 28

After a trying night and week with everything that happened with Calvin and Corey, Elaina was glad to be relaxing on the sofa in the family room with a newspaper in front of her face, on this Saturday afternoon. David was sitting in his favorite spot on the floor doing homework, while Katrina was in a chair near the sofa reading a Seventeen magazine. Everyone was done with their homework for the weekend except David. That was one thing Elaina did not play about; she never played about school work, especially since she was a college professor. And in order to partake in any extracurricular activities on the weekend such as going to the mall or movies with friends, they had to have at least most if not all of their homework done for that weekend.

Elaina lowered the newspaper down, Katrina laid her Seventeen magazine down on her lap, and David stopped doing his homework when they all heard the sound of keys at the front door. They were baffled because the only people who had keys to the house were Elaina, David, Corey, Katrina and Calvin. And Michelle and Darren had a key in case of an emergency. While Elaina, David and Katrina were in the family room, Corey was in his bedroom and Calvin was in Dallas until the end of next week. Darren *was supposed* to be in jail… unless he bonded out.

But that was highly doubtful with all of the charges that were brought against him. And Michelle would only use her key, if Elaina told her to. They watched the doorknob as it turned and the door opened.

"It's Daddy!" David announced and then stood up.

Calvin came inside and set his luggage down by the door.

"You're home early!" Elaina told Calvin, as she folded up her newspaper and set it on the end table.

"Yep!" he replied.

Elaina had a slight smile on her face, forgetting what Michelle showed her, at least for now. She arose from the sofa, walked over to Calvin and gave him a hug. David also walked over to Calvin and gave him a hug, forgetting that his dad missed his championship game… for the moment anyway. Katrina on the other hand, continued reading her Seventeen magazine as if her dad wasn't there. She wasn't so forgiving, just yet.

"How did you manage that?" asked Elaina.

"Well… I called Simon and told him I needed to be at home with my family due to an unforeseen circumstance, and he understood. He's gonna have the other guy go down and finish up the projects."

"Well, you'll get no complaints from me," said Elaina, as she walked back to the sofa and sat down.

"Hey, Baby Girl," Calvin said to Katrina.

"Hey Daddy," she replied as she dropped her magazine down for a second, and then raised it back up to her face.

Calvin sensed his daughter was upset with him, but didn't know why. So, he figured he would leave her alone for now. He asked, "Where's Corey?"

"In his room. This will be a nice surprise for him," Elaina told him.

"Well, let me go check in on him." Calvin headed to Corey's bedroom. When he came up to his bedroom door, he knocked once, and then opened it, peeking his head inside.

Corey said, "Dad!" with a large grin on his face. He had been sitting on his bean bag reading his Ben Carson 'Think Big' book.

"Hey Buddy!" said Calvin as he walked completely into his bedroom.

Corey stood up, sat his book on the dresser and gave his dad a hug. Afterwards, Calvin closed the door behind him. Both of them sat at the foot of Corey's bed.

"I heard what happened."

Corey dropped his head when his dad said that.

Calvin said, "I think I'm the blame for that. I shouldn't have left you guys. I'm sorry, man."

Corey nodded, and said, "I still can't believe he would do something like that. I'm really sorry." Calvin gave his son another hug.

"I think I can get past you not being here, Dad. It's what Uncle Darren did that I'm not so sure about," Corey explained to his dad. "How do you get past the hurt?"

Calvin replied, "Well Corey, I don't know. I'm still learning that myself." Then he took notice of a Bible sitting on Corey's dresser. He stood up, grabbed it, then sat back down on the bed and told Corey, "But I think this will be a good start, and just taking it one day at a time. We'll do it together. What'd you say?"

"Alright," Corey replied as he nodded. Calvin gave his son dap. Corey said, "I'm glad you're back, Dad."

"Me too, son," Calvin responded. He said, "Now, let me go talk to your mom for a moment." He stood up, put the Bible back on Corey's dresser and opened the door.

Corey smiled as his dad walked out. He got up off the bed and grabbed his Bible from the dresser. He looked at it as a thought came to his mind of what Pastor Gillesby told him and his brother. He again smiled to himself.

When Calvin went back into the family room, Elaina, Katrina and David were doing the exact same activities they were doing when Calvin got home.

Calvin said, "Hey David, Trina…" They stopped were they were doing and looked at their dad. "Can you give me and your mom a few moments? I wanna talk to her about something."

"Okay," replied David.

There was no response from Katrina; however, they both got up and left the living room. Calvin came over to the sofa and sat down beside Elaina. Elaina set her newspaper down on the end table as she pondered what he was going to say. David and Katrina actually just stood on the other side of a wall where they couldn't be seen, but could still hear any conversation going on in the living room.

Calvin said, "Laina… I asked Simon to go to Dallas. But only after a little persuasion."

David and Katrina looked at each other when they heard that.

Elaina just said, "Hmm, hmm…" Elaina said to herself, "Keep talking, negro."

"I lied to you when you asked me who I ate with at the restaurant the other night."

Elaina just said, "Hmm, hmm…" Again she was saying to herself, "Keep going," as she folded her arms.

"I had dinner with Patrice that night and the night before…"

Elaina's mouth dropped open slightly as she cocked her head to the side, surprised at what Calvin just told her.

David and Katrina again looked at each other on the other side of the wall.

Calvin quickly said, "But nothing further happened. It was just dinner… I promise."

"I know. Well, correction… I knew about dinner at the restaurant… not about the one you had before," Elaina explained. Then said, "Michelle happened to be in Dallas for a hair show and was eating at that same restaurant when she saw you with her."

"And you didn't say anything? Better yet, *she* didn't say anything?"

"Well, that's only because I told her not to. Oh, she wanted to… believe me. I just knew God would work things out. He always does," she stated.

"Still, if I hadn't decided to go in the first place, none of this would've happened."

Elaina nodded. "Yeah, that's true."

"Including missing David's championship game," said Calvin. Elaina again nodded.

While David murmured, "Yeah, that's true," on the other side of the wall.

161

"I better apologize to him before I'm really in trouble," He told Elaina.

She just continued to nod.

He yelled, "David and Trina, you guys can come back in here." David was getting ready to walk in, but Katrina pulled on his arm.

Katrina murmured, "Wait! We can't go in right away. They'll know we were listening to them the whole time." She and David waited a few more seconds, and then walked into the living room.

Calvin asked, "David, can you forgive me for missing your game?"

"Yeah, I guess so… as long as you don't miss State," he said.

"Oh no, I'm there," Calvin stated and turned his attention to his daughter. "Baby Girl, we good?"

"We good, Daddy," Katrina said with a smile and then gave him a hug. The hug he was supposed to get when he first came into the house.

"Good," replied Calvin.

Chapter 29

*P*astor Gillesby had just preached another powerful message on this Sunday morning, the next day after Calvin had gotten home. It was a full house and just about everyone was attentive except for those few adults and children who were on their devices doing God knows what. The musicians began to play softly. Some in the congregation knew what time it was and bowed their heads, beginning to pray.

"God is calling some of you to a place of complete rest in your heart. That rest begins today. Your healing begins today. You know who you are. God's been tugging at you for a while," Pastor Gillesby asserted, as he slowly scanned the congregation. While some were praying, others were scanning the congregation as well to see who would go up to the altar, even though they should have been praying, also. Calvin, seated among his family, stood up and made his way to the altar.

Elaina at first, looked up at him with astonishment. Then, she smiled, as did the rest of his family. He was dressed in light gray baggy slacks, a pin striped light gray and black long sleeve collar shirt, black cuff links and a black blazer.

Pastor Gillesby said, "Amen! God's been waiting on you. You've been carrying around dead weight for a long time and it's time for you to be free of it."

Calvin nodded. "Can I say something, Pastor?"

"Sure." Pastor Gillesby handed Calvin the microphone. He turned around and faced his family.

"I had to learn the hard way that it's not good to hold on to past hurt. I almost fell in the same trap that caused *my* hurt. It not only tortures you, but also those around you. So… I'm doing this for myself and my family," explained Calvin. He focused his attention on Corey specifically. "I can't help them, if I'm not right myself," Calvin said to him.

Corey nodded as he smiled slightly. Calvin looked out into the congregation. Pastor Gillesby was fine with allowing those at the altar to speak, as long as it was beneficial and necessary for his congregation to hear. There were times though, when he had to take away the microphone from those who got long winded with no reason behind it. This moment was special though, because he was familiar with the Hardy family.

164

Calvin said to the congregation, "Today, I can truly say, I forgive my dad when I thought I never would. Because I, for the first time, felt what it was like to need forgiving. Now I know what my mom was talking about when she told me God gives us mercy over and over again, even when we do wrong." He turned around and gave the microphone back to Pastor Gillesby and said, "Thank you, Pastor."

His family forgot that service was not over yet. They wasted no time in coming to the altar to give Calvin a hug. Elaina looked over at Mother Newsome who was sitting on the second row on the right side with the other mothers of the church, and smiled at her. Mother Newsome returned a smile as she nodded.

Chapter 30

*T*here was a little less than a minute left on the clock of the scoreboard at Montgomery Rose High School. It was the following Saturday. The Carter Academy Eagles were up by six points over the MRHS Tigers. David was at the fifty-yard line when he caught the football thrown to him by the quarterback.

The stands were completely filled with Eagles fans and Tigers fans. Almost everyone was on their feet screaming. With David's size and speed, the Eagles' players were finding it difficult to bring him down. The Tigers' cheerleaders, along with the band were once again in high spirits, getting the fans hyped up and pushing for David to make that touchdown. Along the metal chain link fence hung a large banner that said, 'IV A State Championship'.

David's teammates and coaches eagerly moved down the sideline as he ran with the ball. There were college football scouts hidden among the masses to observe certain players on both teams, mainly seniors.

In the midst of the shouting fans on this rather cool evening, was David's fan club; however, a couple of people were missing. David was okay with that as long as his dad was there this time. And he was, along with his mom, brother and sister. Calvin made sure David knew that, as well as the crowd he sat among.

Calvin shouted, "There it is, son!" toward the field as David crossed the goal line. Then, he announced out loud to the crowd, "That's my boy!" hoping everyone around him heard that. Well it certainly didn't go unnoticed.

A Caucasian man in his late forties turned around to Calvin and said, "Yeah, we know! You said that after his last touchdown." The man was sitting a couple of rows down from Calvin. Calvin frowned at him and sat down for a moment. Elaina, Katrina and Corey all laughed at Calvin.

The scoreboard showed the score as Eagles twenty and Tigers twenty. The time on the clock read ten seconds as the kicker prepared for the extra point. The kicker had everyone's full attention. Just about every fan on both sides of the field were standing. Coach Stevens had his hand over his mouth as he watched his player kick the ball, more than likely silently praying. The Eagles head coach stood with his legs apart and both hands on his hips, hoping the kicker would miss the goal. His hope unfortunately, was a lost cause. The Tigers won. The Eagles fans began leaving as the Tigers celebrated winning the State Championship.

Elaina, Corey and Katrina stayed up in the stands for a while chatting with friends and people they knew, while Calvin made his way down from the stands and walked over to the football field to where the team was. He waited patiently on the sideline while Coach Stevens talked with the team. After the talk, the rowdy players headed off the field along with the coaches.

Calvin walked over to Coach Stevens and shook his hand. David came over and stood by his dad.

"Coach, congratulations on winning your first State Championship!"

Coach Stevens replied, "Thank you. We couldn't have done it without David's help, though. He played a huge part in it. You should be proud of him."

"I am," Calvin said as he looked at David with a smile on his face.

"Keep up the good work, David. We're going to need it again next year."

"Yes, sir," responded David.

Coach Stevens shook David's hand and patted him on the back. David and Calvin left Coach Stevens when other people began coming up to him to congratulate him.

Calvin gave David a pat on the back also while they were walking and told him, "You did awesome, David. I'm really proud of you. I guess you do kind of know what you're doing."

David chuckled a little, and said, "Thanks, Daddy."

While they were walking, a college football scout walked up to David and reached out to shake his hand. David extended his hand out to return the shake.

"David, right?" the football college scout asked.

"Yes, sir."

"I'm a scout from Michigan State," the scout told David and his dad. "I've been coming to watch the senior named Russell play, but I've also noticed you. We'll be keeping an eye on you as well for the next two years. You keep playing the way you're playing; you can definitely have a career in football," he told David.

David looked at his dad with a huge smile. Calvin returned the smile and nodded.

The scout said, "Keep working hard young man." Then left them.

"Maybe a preacher's prayer can work, David," said Calvin.

Chapter 31

*A*n aroma of soul food could be appreciated throughout the Hardy family's home on this particular evening. Elaina had been in her kitchen all day slaving over her hot stove, with a helping hand every now and then from her daughter and husband. The large formal dining table was beautifully set with a burgundy table cloth, the *good* china which only came out every now and then, and two long white candle sticks.

Elaina was dressed in nice casual clothes, as was the rest of her family. She and Katrina placed the food on the table that was set for nine. On the menu was a honey baked ham, perfectly fried chicken, cheesy macaroni & cheese, collard greens, green beans and corn bread muffins. And there was sweet tea with lemon to wash it all down. The dessert for devouring later was a homemade peach cobbler. If your mouth had not watered yet, it should have been by now. Suddenly, the doorbell rang.

Elaina yelled from the kitchen, "Somebody get that!" Her and Katrina's hands were tied up.

David and Corey were already in the family room playing a video game. So, David answered the door.

He yelled, "It's Grandma and Grandpa James... and Aunt Michelle!"

They all came into the house and gave David and Corey a hug. Corey took their jackets and hung them up on the coat rack that was located near the door.

"Where's your mom?" asked Grandma James.

"She's in the kitchen," said Corey. She put her hand on Corey's arm and asked, "How have you been?"

"I've been okay," Corey answered.

"Well, you just take it one day at time, Corey. And let God do the rest. Alright?" she said while Grandpa James stood beside her, nodding.

"Yes, ma'am," replied Corey. Then, she and her husband headed into the kitchen.

"So, what's up, nephews?" Michelle asked.

David said, "No—," before being interrupted by Michelle.

She said quickly, "It sure smells good in here." She headed into the kitchen.

David and Corey laughed at her, and went back to playing their video game. Grandma James began helping with placing the delicious food on the dining table, while Michelle stood at the table eyeing everything.

"Sis… you outdid yourself. Everything looks so good," Michelle told Elaina.

Calvin walked into the dining area where Michelle was, but Michelle didn't see him come in. He stood there for a moment watching her as she admired all the food.

Calvin said, "No thanks to you."

Michelle turned around and rolled her eyes at him. "Hey C.J," she said softly, as Calvin passed her to go into the entrance between the kitchen and dining area. Then she said to him, "Don't forget… you still on my bad list."

Elaina met him at the entrance as she placed a basket of corn muffins on the table.

"I'll always be on your bad list if it's up to you," Calvin replied.

Elaina murmured, "Calvin!" as she shook her head. Then, she said quickly, "Thanks, Michelle," to end that conversation before it got out of hand.

Calvin went into the kitchen and spoke to Elaina's parents.

Elaina yelled, "Time to eat, guys!" That was meant for everyone.

Corey and David had no problem hearing 'time to eat'; they were just hard of hearing when it came to doing certain chores around the house. Everyone began sitting

172

down at the table as they gawked over all the food. Calvin sat at one end of the table, and on the right side of the table was Elaina, Katrina and Grandma James. Elaina was seated beside her husband as her mom was beside her husband at the other end of the table. Michelle sat on the left side beside her dad, David beside her, and Corey beside David. Everyone was more than ready to dig in.

Elaina asked, "Calvin, can you bless the food, please?"

"Yes, be glad to," he responded with a slight smile. Everyone bowed their heads. He prayed, "Lord, thank you for this time of fellowship with my family. Even the not so favorite one." Calvin raised his head and looked over at Michelle. Michelle raised her head because she knew he was talking about her, and she gave him a mean smirk. Everyone else raised their heads and looked at Calvin. He continued by saying, "But… we learn to love them anyway." Calvin gave Michelle a slight smile as she returned a slight one back at him. Everyone else either smiled or snickered, then, bowed their heads again. The grace continued with, "Bless my beautiful wife who prepared this delicious food," Elaina smiled slightly. "and may it be nourishment to our bodies. And Lord… thank you for new beginnings in this family. Amen."

All could be heard next was, "pass the chicken, pass the mac and cheese, pass the ham…," as everyone began piling it on.

Then, the doorbell rang. Everyone paused only for a second. Calvin said, "You guys can go ahead and eat. I'll see who it is." He got up from the table and headed to the front door. After he took a quick look through the peep hole, he opened the door. A somewhat tall, African-American man in his early seventies stood there dressed in a dark navy blue wind breaker type jacket, some dark brown baggy slacks and a rather nice polo type shirt, along with a complementing fedora hat. He had a few wrinkles in his face and a slight overlap in the belly. They both were frozen for a moment as they made eye contact. "Dad."

"Hi, Junior," said Calvin Sr. "Glad you could make it," Calvin told his dad. Then, said, "Well, come in… come in."

When he stepped inside of the house, Calvin gave him a hug, before his dad took off his jacket, and then his fedora, revealing his salt and pepper colored hair.

"Here, let me take your jacket and hat," he said to his dad, and then hung his jacket and hat on the coat rack.

Calvin Sr. began surveying his son's home.

"Nice home you got here, son."

"Thank you."

"Thanks for having me," said Calvin Sr.

174

"Well, it's been long overdue," he said to his dad.

Calvin Sr. unveiled his gratitude with a slight smile.

His son said, "I'll take you into the dining room and introduce you to everyone. We were just starting to eat." Everyone at the table paused from eating when Calvin walked into the dining area with his dad. You would think everyone had seen a ghost. Everyone except for Grandma James, Grandpa James and Michelle knew that it would be a possibility his dad would show up. No one had met him yet, and Calvin had only been communicating with him over the phone for the past couple of weeks. He announced, "Everyone... this is my dad, Calvin Hardy Sr."

Elaina stood up, walked over to him and gave him a hug. She said, "Welcome, Dad. We've been saving a seat just for you."

There was an empty seat beside Calvin's seat, right across from Elaina on the left side of the table. Calvin pulled out the chair for his dad. Elaina sat back down in her seat, and then Calvin and his dad sat down.

Calvin said, "Well Dad, dig in whenever you're ready."

Calvin Sr. quickly surveyed what was on the table and moved the cloth napkin off of his empty plate. "I think I will. I've been waiting for this moment," he told his son. Then, he said, "Somebody pass that fried chicken please."

Everyone chuckled while they stuffed their faces. When the chicken was passed to him, he grabbed a leg off of it and put the plate down in front of him. He proceeded to take a bite, but remembered he hadn't said his grace yet. He took a quick peek down the table to see if anyone saw him, then, bowed his head for a hot second and took that bite before he grabbed other food items to put on his plate. He didn't realize that his son and daughter-in-law had already been eyeing him. They snickered underneath their breath.

"Well Dad, I know you'll have time to get to know everyone after we eat, but I'll do a quick introduction," Calvin told his dad.

Calvin Sr. said, "Well, I know these are my grandchildren. That beautiful young lady sitting by your wife must be Katrina." Katrina nodded and smiled. "And from what I can remember from the picture you sent me, this is Doctor Corey sitting here beside me and the future NFL player beside him. Right, David?" he said, as he looked at them and continued to eat in between talking.

"Yes, sir," David confirmed proudly.

Calvin said, "And beside David, is my wife's baby sister, Michelle."

"I prefer *youngest* sister, please," insisted Michelle.

Calvin looked at her with a straight face, while Elaina just dropped her head down. Their mom and dad shook their heads. Calvin's dad chuckled, as well as the kids.

Calvin nodded toward the other end of the table and said, "And that's Fred and Norma James, Elaina and Michelle's parents."

"Good to meet everybody. And Elaina... you sho know how to cook. I haven't had a good meal like this in a while," said Calvin Sr.

"Thank you," she said, as she smiled.

Chapter 32

*W*ith full stomachs, Calvin and his dad sat at a table on his closed in patio to take some precious time to get to know each other again. Elaina's parents and sister had gone home. Corey and David were playing video games, while Elaina and Katrina cleaned up the kitchen.

"You know, Junior... I thought I would never hear from you again. I know I really hurt you and your mom back then, but it was never my intention," he explained to his son.

"I can come to understand that now, Dad, but back then, all I could see were lies."

Elaina came out on the patio and asked, "You two want any coffee before I close down the kitchen?"

"You want some, Dad?" Calvin asked again because he hadn't responded yet. He was still hung up on what his son said.

Calvin Sr. finally responded, "Uh, yeah, I'll take some coffee."

"I'll just take some more tea, Sugar Plum," said Calvin.

Elaina quickly bent down to his ear and said to her husband, "Don't call me that in front of your dad," she whispered. She stood straight up and left to fetch their drinks.

"As I was saying, Dad… I've come to accept that the past is just that. We can't change what happened, but we can learn from our mistakes and move forward," explained Calvin.

His dad replied, "Yeah, you right, Junior," as he nodded.

"So, what have you been up to for all these years, Dad?"

"Well… I retired from the construction business about four years ago. Now, all I do is go fishing every now and then with a couple of buddies, play a little golf to stay in shape and go to church," his dad said, as Elaina brought out their drinks.

She sat down Calvin Sr.'s coffee in front of him first. "Thank you, Laina."

"You're welcome, Dad." Then, she sat down her husband's tea in front of him.

"Thank you, Sugar Plum," Calvin said.

Elaina murmured, "Calvin!" as she nudged him on his arm before leaving the patio. All he did was smile to himself. His dad chuckled a bit.

"You got a good one there, Junior. Hold on to her."

"Yeah... don't I know. She had every right to kick me out a few weeks ago," said Calvin. "That's one reason why I felt it was time to forgive you. That doggone devil sure is good at setting traps up for us men."

"Yeah, he is, son," his dad confirmed, as he chuckled. "You talking about that situation you told me about when you were in Dallas?"

"Yeah," Calvin responded while nodding.

"Well, I'm glad everything worked out."

"Yeah... but I'm having the darnest time forgiving myself for what happened to Corey. If I hadn't left, that would've never happened."

"That may be true, but he was bound to be exposed sooner or later, Junior. It's good that Corey spoke up about it."

"Yeah, I'm glad he did."

"Junior, I really enjoyed myself this evening. You don't know how much I prayed for this," Calvin Sr. told his son, while finishing off the last bit of coffee he had in his cup. Then he stood up. "My eyes are not what they used to be. So, I'm gone go ahead and hit the road while it's not too late. That way I can make it home in one piece."

"Yeah, Dad, you do that," Calvin said, as he stood up from the table as well. "You probably not supposed to be doing much driving at night anyway, are you?"

Calvin Sr. responded, "No... not really."

"That's what I thought," Calvin said while laughing. "Come on, I'll walk you out."

Chapter 33

"**Y**ou talked to Tony since you've been back?" Elaina asked Calvin while they sat at the table on their patio. Calvin continued sipping on his tea.

"No, not yet," he answered. "Not sure what to say to him."

"Well, you shouldn't let a home wrecker ruin you guys relationship." Calvin was without words as he sat with his hand wrapped around his glass of tea, gazing at it. Elaina said, "Just call him, babe. You'll know what to say when you call."

"Yeah... alright," he responded while he nodded. Then, he took his cell phone out of his pocket and placed it on the table. He cupped his hand over his mouth as he contemplated what he was going to say to Tony.

"Oh, you're getting ready to call now?"

"There's no time like the present."

"You're right," Elaina told him as she nodded. "I'll give you some privacy. If I stay out here, I'll be trying to tell you what to say."

"I don't care if you stay."

"No, you have to be the one to clean this up," she said, as she got up from the table. "You want me to take this in?" Elaina placed her hand around Calvin's glass siting on the table. It was pretty much empty except for the ice that had melted into the drop of tea left at the bottom of the glass.

"Yeah, that's fine," he replied.

She picked up his glass before she left him alone. Calvin held his phone in his hand for a moment while he stared into space. He finally bit the bullet.

"Oh, now you decide to call me?" asked Tony, when he answered Calvin's call.

"T.B., wait... I'm calling to say sorry, man. I didn't mean for any of this to happen," Calvin explained. "I admit... I got caught up, but nothing happened between us."

"How'd you end up in Dallas anyway?" asked Tony.

"We started some development projects there, and I asked to head them up."

"So, Patrice knew you were coming?"

"No, she didn't. She knew we were gonna be starting a couple of projects there, but she didn't know I would be over them until I emailed her." There was complete silence from Tony. "When I saw her at the office in Dallas, she invited me to stop by her place."

"And you just had to take her up on the offer, huh?"

"I just didn't think it would be a problem at the time," Calvin said. "Now I know it was a problem from the moment I went to the cafeteria with her."

"Uh… you think, C.J.? And I take it, Laina found out?"

"Yeah."

"How'd that happen, because I didn't tell her."

"Her sister was at the same restaurant where Patrice and I had dinner."

"Michelle? And you two went out to eat?"

"That's a positive on both," Calvin answered as he closed his eyes, finding it hard to tell his friend about going out to dinner, too.

On the other end, Tony grabbed his forehead with his free hand and shook his head.

"Man C.J., you want to have your cake and eat it too, leaving nothing but crumbs for little 'ol Tony!"

"Naw, man. It's not like that."

"Apparently it is," said Tony. "And what was Michelle doing in Dallas?"

"She was there for a hair show."

"Man, I told you… God has a way of exposing stuff."

"Yeah, I see that," Calvin responded. "I just wish I'd never gone in the first place. You remember Darren?"

"The one Laina calls her brother?"

"Yeah. I had him bringing Corey home from the center he worked at while I was out of town, and turns out he's been molesting kids, man!"

"You're kidding, right?"

"No. He put his hands on Corey," Calvin said.

"What? And you didn't kill him?"

"Trust me... I wanted to," answered Calvin, as he stood up from the table and began moving around. "Laina had him arrested before I came home. I think that was the best thing to do or I'd be in prison right now."

Elaina came to the sliding door to see if Calvin was still on the phone, but didn't open it since she saw that he was.

"Yeah, you would. How's Corey taking this?"

When Calvin glanced over at her, she gave him a thumbs up with the question displayed on her face: How are things going?

Calvin returned a thumbs up to her. She nodded and walked away from the sliding door.

"He's working through it; one day at a time. We all are," Calvin replied.

"Man, C.J., that's sick."

"The really sick part to me is that he was family to us," said Calvin.

"Yeah, man. I'm really sorry that happened."

"I am too. We'll get through it, though, with God's help."

"What'd you say?"

"I said, we'll get through it, though, with God's help."

"I thought I heard you say, 'with God's help.' Are you a church man now?" asked Tony.

Calvin let out a quick laugh as he remembered asking Tony that same question before. "Let's just say… I've come to see how important it is to have Him in my life."

Tony smiled on the other end as he nodded. Calvin asked, "So, T.B… is the air clear between you and me?"

"Man, you know we been through too much to let a female come in between us," he told Calvin. "And you know, you don't have any other friends really."

Calvin just laughed. "So, you gone try to see Patrice again?" asked Calvin.

"Naw… I don't mess with women who're into flirting with married men."

They both chuckled a little.

"Well, I'll catch up with you soon, T.B."

"Alright, C.J. Glad you called."

"Me too. Later, man," Calvin told him before hanging up. He walked into the house heading to his and Elaina's bedroom. When he walked inside, Elaina was dressed in comfortable pajamas and sitting up in bed, enjoying a book.

"Well, how did it go?" asked Elaina, who was dying to find out how Calvin's call went.

"It's all good."

"Thank God," she said.

Chapter 34

*I*t was around 8:30 on this rather cold, slightly foggy morning of January when Calvin decided to take a detour from his regular route to work. He pulled up alongside a curb in his Range Rover, then got out. He was dressed in a pair of quality black slacks, a white long sleeve collar shirt, a complementing tie, and a black coat. He had a bouquet of fresh white calla lilies in his hand as he walked not far from his vehicle to a tombstone that displayed 'Rose Lillian Hardy, Rest In Peace Beloved' along with a pair of praying hands. He removed the dead flowers, before he laid down the lilies. These was his mom's favorite flower.

"Hey, Momma. I know it's been a while since I've been by to see you," he said. "Sorry about that. It's been a little hectic for the last two months. And completely crazy this month, which is why I stopped by. I have some good news and some bad news to tell you. I'll tell you the bad news first." There was such a stillness in the air as Calvin stood alone in the cemetery. The sun was beginning to peek out a little. He said, "I messed up real bad." He began to weep a little, then said, "I made a decision that put Corey in danger. And I almost did what dad did to you." He started wiping his tears. "Everything is okay now, but it's just that... he wouldn't've had to go through what he went through, if I hadn't made the decision I made."

Calvin pulled himself back together. "The good news is that you'll be proud to know I finally forgave dad for what he did to you. And... I rededicated my life to God. That should make you smile," he said. The sun was shining a little brighter now. Calvin took a white handkerchief out of his coat pocket and dried his face. "Well, I have to get going or I won't have a job. I love you, Momma. I'll see you soon." He kissed the inside of his fingers, then touched his mom's tombstone. He took his sunglasses out of his coat pocket, and slipped them on as he walked back to his vehicle. He got inside, started it up and drove off.

When Calvin arrived at work, he proceeded straight to his office, closed his door slightly and tackled some paperwork. This week happened to be one of the two weeks Patrice was in town. While walking in the hallway, she glanced in the window and saw him sitting at his desk. Calvin was deep into his work with his head down and didn't see her. She knocked on the door and then peeked her head in.

Calvin raised his head up. "Patrice."

"Hey," she said and came into his office. She began closing the door.

Calvin told her quickly, "No, you can leave it open."

"So, you had to leave Dallas earlier than planned?"

"Yeah. Who told you?" asked Calvin.

"I asked someone at the Dallas office when I hadn't seen you around. Did something happen?"

"Yeah, I just had some things that needed taken care of at home that were more important. So, my boss sent my associate down there to finish the projects," explained Calvin.

"Well, I hope everything is okay now."

"It is. Thanks for asking."

"You're welcome to join me for lunch today."

"No, I better not, Patrice," he told her. "I actually shouldn't have joined you when I did before, I shouldn't have taken you to the airport without telling my wife and I really didn't have any business going to Dallas like I did."

Patrice turned her head sideways at Calvin as she looked perplexed. "What are you saying?" asked Patrice, as she sat down in one of his chairs in front of his desk.

"I'm saying, I love my wife and I want my wife to continue loving me. So our relationship, will be strictly business."

"Oh... I see," she responded, as she dropped her head down. She stood up.

"Patrice, you're a beautiful woman, but you're not worth losing my family over... at least not for me."

She was taken by his comment. "Well Mr. Hardy, it was fun while it lasted. I guess I'll see you around," Patrice said before walking out of Calvin's office.

He sat back in his chair and then turned around to the window facing downtown as he focused his attention outside. He smiled as he said to himself, "Way to handle that, Calvin."

Chapter 35

*E*laina, while in the kitchen, heard her cell phone ring. She came into the family room where her purse was sitting on the sofa, reached inside and grabbed her phone. She looked at the number to see if she recognized it, then shrugged and answered it.

"Hello?"

"Is this Elaina Hardy?"

"Yes," she answered while sitting on the sofa.

"My name is Elizabeth Starison. I'm calling from the District Attorney's office to let you know that Darren Border will be sentenced on Friday, January 16th at 10:30 a.m."

"Okay."

"You're welcome to attend if you desire. Also the judge will allow you five minutes to address the defendant as well, if you desire."

"Okay. Ms. Starison, do you mind if I put you on hold while I grab something to write on?"

"Sure, no problem."

Elaina took her cell phone away from her ear as she walked into her bedroom to grab a notepad, then came back into the family room, and sat back down on the sofa.

"Thank you for being patient. Now, did you say Friday, January 16th?" Elaina asked while she grabbed a pen from her purse.

Moments later, Calvin walked in and placed his keys and briefcase on a table near the family room.

"Yes, ma'am. Will you be in attendance?"

Elaina wrote the information down and answered, "Yes, I plan on being there."

"Who's that?" Calvin mouthed to Elaina.

She held up her 'one moment' finger to him.

"Okay. Do you have an email address so we can send you all of the details?" Ms. Starison asked.

"Yes, I do. It's ejhardy5259@gmail.com."

"Great, thank you. We'll send you an email out this week.

"Thank you for notifying us."

"No problem. And if you have any additional questions before then, feel free to call our office."

"I will," Elaina said and hung up.

"Who was that?" asked Calvin.

"That was the District Attorney's office. Darren is being sentenced on next Friday. So, they were notifying us," she explained. "I plan on going."

"You need for me to go?"

"That's up to you."

"Yeah. If you're going, I think I need to be there with you."

"And, I'll let Corey decide if he wants to go. I doubt he will," said Elaina. Then, she yelled, "Hey, Corey!"

Calvin began looking through the mail lying on the end table. Corey and David came into the family room.

"I thought I just called Corey... not Corey *and* David. I called Corey so I can ask him a question."

David turned around and headed back out. It was presumed by his mom that he would be returning back to his bedroom; however instead, he stood on the other side of the wall hidden from Calvin, Elaina and Corey.

"Ma'am?" answered Corey, while he stood in front of his mom.

"Darren is going to be sentenced on next Friday. The victims can come and say something if they want. Your dad and I will be going. Did you want to go?" Corey stood there for a moment, pondering if he should go or not. Elaina said, "Sweetheart, you don't have to go if you don't want to. I figured I'd let you make your own decision." She could already tell he didn't want to.

"Yeah... I'm not ready to face him again yet."

Elaina replied, "That's perfectly fine, son."

"Yeah, that's understandable. We'll stand in for you," Calvin told his son while giving him a pat on the back.

"Thank you," replied Corey.

"You can go back to your room," Elaina told Corey.

Corey walked out of the room, and found David standing by the wall.

"What are you doing?" whispered Corey.

"Standing nearby just in case she needed me, too," whispered David as they both walked to their bedrooms.

"If she needed you, she would have called you. You just wanted to be nosey."

"That's possible," answered David while nodding.

Chapter 36

*I*t was a very busy atmosphere with people coming and going from the Oakland County Circuit Court located in Pontiac, Michigan. Some were dressed nice, while others could easily wear a stamp across their forehead that said, 'Criminal'. The court was about twenty-five minutes away from Southfield. The time was about 10 a.m. Elaina and Calvin was waiting patiently in line to go through the metal detectors. They finally reached the actual detector. Elaina put her purse and cell phone in the bin while Calvin placed his keys and cell phone in it as well. They walked through the metal detector without alarm as the bin passed through on the moving belt. Once through, the security person informed them that they would be able to get their cell phones back before they left. They were not happy about that, as they were unaware cell phones were prohibited from inside of the court.

Never the less, they proceeded to the elevators so they could arrive in the courtroom on time. Inside the courtroom where Darren would be sentenced, there were about fifteen people scattered around. There were five people sitting on the right side of the courtroom and six on the left that consisted of men, women, African-American and Caucasian. The bailiff stood by a door on the left hand side, up at the front of the courtroom, and the courtroom secretary sat at a desk not far from the bailiff, typing up information from the last session. Elaina and Calvin took a seat on the second row, on the left hand side.

Not long after they sat down, the District Attorney, a Caucasian woman in her mid to late thirties, walked into the courtroom carrying her briefcase over to an empty table sitting on the right side in front of the church-like bench. Next the door opened where the bailiff was standing and in walked Darren dressed in a dark green jump suit following behind his attorney, a Caucasian man in his mid-forties. He wasn't detained in any handcuffs or shackles since he didn't pose as a direct threat to anyone. He and his lawyer sat at an empty table located on the left side in front of the church-like bench.

Elaina and Calvin looked upon him with disgrace and disgust. Moments later, the door right beside the bench on the right side of the courtroom opened. Judge Meredith Holmes, an African-American woman in her early fifties stepped into the courtroom. Her demeanor displayed years of experience and one who was not to be reckoned with. She stepped up to the bench, sat down and placed the dark brown folders she was carrying on the desk. She began reviewing the pre-sentence report. She grabbed the gavel and hit it on the sound block. After all necessary salutations were addressed, the actual hearing began.

"Will the defendant please rise and state your true birth name?" asked Judge Holmes.

"Darren Nathan Border."

"And your date of birth?"

"September 20th, 1973."

"Thank you. On December 4th, two thousand and fourteen, the state found you guilty on eight counts of child sexual abuse and eight counts of indecent exposure to minors. It's now time for entering judgement and sentence. For all eight counts, it is the judgement of the court that defendant, Darren Nathan Border, is guilty of the crimes stated at hand," explained Judge Holmes. "The court has considered all of the evidence presented at different phases of the trial. A sentencing memorandum was received from the defendant. I show the defendant has been in custody for fifty-three days. Is that correct, Counsel?"

"That is correct," answered Darren's attorney.

"Thank you. You may be seated at this time." Judge Holmes then focused her attention on the D.A.

"Ms. Rundure, do any of the victims wish to be heard?"

"Yes, they do. The parents of two of the minors involved."

"Very well. Let's proceed."

"The first of the two who will be addressing the court, is Ms. June Matthews, a mother of one of the victims," informed Ms. Rundure.

"Ms. Matthews, please come forward and state your full name to the court," Judge Holmes requested.

Ms. Matthews approached a podium located right in between the attorney's tables. She was an African-American woman of average height, who appeared to be in her early thirties.

"My name is June Evette Matthews. Your Honor. I come on behalf of my fourteen-year-old son, Kenny Matthews. I just recently found out that this monster was molesting my child. Kenny never said anything about it, and now I know why. He was bribing these kids with tickets to games," Ms. Matthews explained, then began shedding tears. "Your Honor... it's just me trying to raise him by myself. His dad has never been his life. I entrusted Mr. Border with my son in hopes of him being a father figure to him. And he violated that trust. He stripped him of the manhood that was developing in him!"

Elaina dropped her head down and shook it. She was empathetic toward Ms. Matthews.

"Please give him the max sentence he's able to get. He doesn't belong on the streets. Thank you." Ms. Matthews said. She wiped her face and walked back to her seat.

"Thank you for your statement," Judge Holmes said.

"Next, is Mr. and Mrs. Calvin Hardy, Jr.," said Ms. Rundure. Elaina and Calvin stood up and approached the podium.

"State your full names individually to the court, please," Judge Holmes requested.

"My name is Elaina Victoria Hardy."

"And I'm Calvin Bernard Hardy, Jr."

"Your Honor… we're here on behalf of our sixteen-year-old son, Corey Hardy, as well as those victims' parents who were not able to come. This has been extremely hard on my family because Darren was like a brother to me and an uncle to my children," explained Elaina.

Darren dropped his head down.

"So I don't understand why he would do this to my son and the other kids. Corey is so hurt by this that he can't even face Darren. He was welcomed in my parents' home growing up and our home, as family. I just don't get it!"

Calvin could sense that Elaina was getting upset, so he grabbed her hand. She looked over at Darren whose head was still down. "I want you to know, Darren, I forgive you for what you did. And I pray God deals with you while you're behind bars. I'm not gonna say what sentence you deserve. It's God's wrath you have to worry about," said Elaina, and she looked back up at the judge. "Thank you, your Honor." Elaina continued to hold on to Calvin's hand as they walked back to their seats.

"Thank you for your statement. Are there any other statements that need to be made, Counsel?"

"No, there's not," said Ms. Rundure.

Judge Holmes asked Darren's attorney, "Will the defendant be making a statement?"

Darren's attorney whispered in Darren's ear. Darren shook his head. Then his attorney said, "No, he will not."

The D.A and defendant's counsel were given time to make their closing statements.

"Is there any legal cause why sentence should not be announced today?" asked Judge Holmes.

"All clear," both counsels responded.

"The court has considered the circumstances and nature of the offense. I've considered all of the complicating and mitigating factors also found by the jury and have identified all of those factors myself, in arriving at a sentence for Mr. Border," Judge Holmes stated.

Mr. Border and his attorney were already standing. She stated each of the complicating and mitigating factors to the court. Then she said, "It is ordered by the court, that the defendant shall be incarcerated in the Department of Corrections for the rest of his natural life with no possibility of parole. The sentence will begin on today. The defendant shall receive credit for the fifty-three days already served," Judge Holmes continued with closing remarks and instructions. Court was adjourned.

Elaina and Calvin watched as the officers took Darren out of the courtroom. Before leaving out of the room, Darren looked over at Elaina and mouthed, "Sorry," to her. She just stared at him as he left out of the door.

Chapter 37

*E*laina and Calvin entered through the front door of their home exhausted and drained. Corey lowered the book he was reading. He sat in one of his favorite chairs where he liked to read in the corner of the family room. David was in his favorite spot on the floor watching T.V. and Katrina, in her bedroom on the phone as usual.

Elaina walked over to the sofa and plopped down. She took her shoes off and put them aside.

"Mom, what happened?" asked Corey.

"I'll tell you, but all at one time," Elaina replied.

Calvin sat down beside Elaina. Then he asked, "Where's Trina?"

"In her bedroom," answered David.

She yelled, "Trina!"

Katrina yelled, "Ma'am?" after peeking her head out of her bedroom door.

"Come here, please," Elaina shouted.

Katrina finally made her way into the family room. "Bout time. Momma only called you like yesterday," David told his sister.

"Shut up, David and mind you!" Katrina said.

"Alright, alright," Elaina intervened before things got out of hand. "I called you in here so I can tell all of you at the same time what happened with Darren. He was sentenced to life in prison."

"Meaning... he'll never get out of prison?" David asked.

"Well, as of right now... no," answered Calvin.

"Wow!" exclaimed Katrina.

Corey was without words.

Elaina asked, "Corey, you alright?"

"Yes ma'am," Corey replied. "I just didn't expect for him to get life."

Elaina asked, "You thought he should've received something worst?"

"No."

"He's blessed that Michigan doesn't have the death penalty because I believe Kenny's mom would have asked for it," Elaina said.

Calvin asserted, "Yeah, that's true."

"You know what we need to do now?" asked Elaina.

David answered, "Forget we ever knew him, right?"

Elaina and Calvin chuckled.

"Boy, no," Elaina replied. "We need to pray for him; for protection and that he comes to know God while he's in there. Who knows... he may be able to get out of there early if he has good behavior."

"What's going to happen to the center?" asked Corey.

Elaina said, "Nothing. They still have adults to run it. "Why, you're thinking about going again?"

"No," Corey answered quickly.

"That's fine," Calvin told him. "Well... I have a surprise for you and David."

"What is it?" David asked.

"I thought this would be a nice activity for us to do and help get your mind off of Darren, Corey. We are going fishing with my dad in the morning."

"Fishing? But we've never been fishing," David said.

Calvin replied, "I know. That's why it should be fun."

"Okay, cool," said Corey.

"Well, when are *we* gonna do something together, Daddy?" Katrina asked.

Calvin asked, "What is it you wanna do, Trina?"

"Shopping," she replied, as Corey and David mouthed it at the same time.

Elaina chuckled a little because she knew the answer to that as well. They all knew exactly what she was going to say, including Calvin.

"How about I give you the money to go shopping?" Calvin asked. "Then you and your mom can go together."

"Yeah, sure, that works for me, too."

"Of course it does… every time," Calvin said, as he smiled at his daughter. She smiled back at him. Calvin said, "Well… I guess we need to go get a few things for our fishing trip in the morning. Let me change clothes and we'll head out," Calvin told Corey and David and walked out of the living room.

"This should be hilarious!" Katrina said while giggling. "You guys don't know anything about fishing."

"Ha, ha, ha," said David.

Corey told his sister, "Well, I bet you won't put your mouth on any of the fish we bring home."

"That's *if* you bring any home," said Katrina.

Elaina said, "Trina, leave your brothers alone."

Chapter 38

*T*he birds were chirping and you could hear the sounds of animals scurrying throughout the bushes along the lake. It was such a serene atmosphere on that early morning. The sun was not quite out yet; making it a rather cold morning. Calvin Sr. slowly cruised around in his burgundy Pro Guide Tracker boat, as he kept an eye on the fish finder to locate a good spot for fishing.

David yelled, "Hello!" His 'Hello' echoed throughout the lake.

"Shh... you gone run the fish away," his granddad told him. They were all dressed in rugged jeans or khakis and thick long sleeve fleeces. They also wore hats and life jackets. Their fishing poles were in their hands, ready to throw out once given the word.

"Let's try this spot," said Calvin Sr. He stopped the boat and stood up from his seat. "Junior, hand me that white

207

Styrofoam bucket sitting behind you. After handing the bucket to his dad, he opened it and put the top on the floor.

Corey and David watched with wide eyes. His dad pulled out a long, wiggly earth worm covered in dirt. "This is what we gone start out using to fish," said Calvin Sr.

David asked nervously, "Who's touching that?"

"I'll take it, Granddad, since Mr. Goody Two-Shoes is scared of it." Corey quickly grabbed the worm from his granddad.

"Here… let me see your pole. I'll show you how to put him on the hook."

Calvin watched his dad also, then grabbed a worm for himself and put it on the hook of his pole while David continued to watch from afar.

David said, "I'm not scared, Corey." Then asked, "Granddaddy, you have any gloves?"

His dad laughed at him while he dropped his line in the water. Corey dropped his in the water also. The sun was just now finding its way out.

"Lift that seat up, David. There may be a pair in there," his granddad said.

It was the seat that his dad sat in, closer to the back of the boat. David raised up the seat and inside were fishing tools, a pack of hooks, different lures, pliers and lo and behold… a pair of work gloves. David took them out and put them on. They were a little too big, but he didn't care as long as his hands didn't touch the worms. Everyone was snickering at him as they watched. He finally reached in the bucket and grabbed a worm. His granddad asked, "You need me to help you put it on the hook, David?"

"No, sir. I think I got it." David struggled somewhat; he was beginning to squeeze the worm to death with the gloves. Although half dead, he managed to finally put the worm on his hook. He dropped his line into the water. His dad and brother continued to snicker as they watched him.

"Oh, oh!" Corey said, as his pole began to bend. "I think I have something, Dad!"

"Start reeling it in," his granddad told him.

Corey began to do just as he said. Then his granddad said, "Not too fast, though."

As he continued to reel in, it was easy to distinguish that he had a fish on his pole. Corey pulled it in closer and held it up out of the water.

"Look at that, Corey! You caught your first yellow perch! A good size too," his granddad told him.

Corey grinned from ear to ear. "I like this!" he said, before he asked, "We can eat him, right?"

"You sure can. That's good eating!" replied his granddad.

"Wait until Trina sees this," Corey said, as he continued looking at his fish.

It was obvious David was a little jealous. He sucked his teeth as he looked at Corey's fish.

Calvin said, "Good job, Corey."

"I'm next," David said. "And mine is gone be bigger."

"Alright, David. Put your money where your mouth is," his dad told him.

Seconds later, Calvin's pole began to bend. "Hold up! Something's on my pole!" He reeled in his line, finding a nice rainbow trout on the end of it.

"That's a nice trout you got there, son. Let me measure it to make sure we can keep it, though," his dad said. Calvin Sr. put his pole down while his son took the trout off of his hook. His dad grabbed the fish and laid it flat beside the ruler on the cooler. "Look like it's about 7 1/2 inches long. Close enough," his dad said and placed the trout inside the cooler.

"How long does it have to be in order to keep it?" Calvin asked his dad.

"Eight inches. We'll be fine as long as the man don't come around snooping."

"Who's 'the man'?" asked David.

"The Wildlife Resource Officer," replied his granddad.

"Oh," David said.

Calvin Jr., Corey and David all looked at him with worried faces.

"We don't have nothing to worry about. They don't come out on the water this early," Calvin Sr. explained.

They all sighed.

Suddenly, David's eyes got big and he said, "Hey… my pole is bending!" as he began reeling his line in. While reeling, he tilted to the left, then to the right. He was working really hard to pull in his fish.

"Look like you may have something big, David," said his dad. "He just might beat us, Corey."

"I think so," David answered as he began to stumble a little.

"You got it, son?" asked his granddad. All eyes were focused on David's pole.

"Yes… sir."

"Look like he *may* beat us, Dad," Corey said.

David continued to fight and reel in whatever was on the end of his line. He finally got it to the boat and lifted it up.

David yelled, "What… a stick!"

Everyone bust out in a laugh except for David.

"That's some catch you got there, Bro."

"Shut up, Corey! I don't like this fishing."

"Don't give up on it yet, David," his granddad told him in hopes of him catching a fish before the end of their fishing trip.

Calvin told his son, "Yeah, I'm sure you'll catch a fish soon."

David unraveled the line from around the stick and threw the stick far out to the side of the boat. Then, he just sat there holding his pole.

Calvin said, "David... you're not gone catch anything if your line is not in the water."

David grabbed the gloves and dug out another worm. He put the worm on his hook and threw his line back into the water. This time he managed not to squeeze his worm half to death.

By the end of the fishing trip, David did end up catching a few fish, but not as big as Corey's. That made David kind of jealous. In all, they had caught five rainbow trout and six yellow perch. Calvin Sr. began driving the boat back in to the dock. He said, "It was a good day."

"Yeah, we're not going home empty handed," Calvin said, as he looked inside of the cooler. Then he said, "Dad, you can come over while we fry these at the house?"

"Sounds good to me."

Corey said, "Granddad, thanks for taking us fishing."

"You're welcome, Corey."

"Dad, you were right. This did take my mind off of… you know," said Corey.

"Good. I'm sure we'll do it again soon," Calvin replied, as he tapped Corey on the arm with his elbow. He looked at David. "Right, David?"

"Well, I don't think this fishing thing is for me. I'll just stick to football and just stay home next time."

Corey said, "Well, at least Trina can't rub it in our faces that we didn't catch anything."

"That's true. And she's not allowed to eat any either," replied David.

They arrived back at home, bringing the cooler of fish into the garage, then knocked on the door leading into the house.

Elaina opened the door for them. "Whew! You guys smell like sweat and fish, all rolled up in one. Please hurry and take a bath," she told her husband and sons as they came into the house. She yelled after them, "And please… do not touch a thing in the house until you bathe." She stepped into the garage and walked over to the cooler, looking inside. She said, "Hmm… not bad."

"I see you being nosey," Calvin told Elaina as he stood at the garage door leading into the house. He surprised her. He said, "I was coming to tell you that I'll take a bath after I clean the fish."

Elaina asked, "What's the rush?"

"We're frying those suckers up tonight," said Calvin. "My dad is coming over to eat some too."

"Oh, okay," replied Elaina. Calvin stayed in the garage while Elaina walked back inside the house. Then yelled, "Trina, they caught some fish!"

Trina was in the living room watching T.V. "Dang! Now, I'll have to hear about it," Trina said to herself.

Elaina yelled, "Your brothers may be nice enough to let you eat some because that's what we're having for dinner."

"Great," Trina whispered once again to herself.

Chapter 39

"**Y**ou know; I've been thinking... I believe it's time for me to pay someone a visit," Calvin said as he cut a piece of his sausage on his plate and placed it in his mouth. He and Elaina were enjoying breakfast together at the kitchen table on a Saturday in the beginning of May, which consisted of eggs, sausage links, biscuits and orange juice. The kids had already eaten and were busy either doing chores or homework.

She asked, "Who?"

"Darren."

"Really?"

"Yeah. I think it's time for me to ask him some questions I've been wondering about. I couldn't do it six months ago, Laina. I would've killed him if I had the chance," Calvin said, as he stuffed his mouth with eggs.

"Oh, I know," Elaina confirmed. "When are you going?"

"Sometime this week. I'm gonna call the Department of Corrections and set it up."

"Okay," said Elaina while nodding. She was feeling somewhat concerned, although she wouldn't come out and say it. She asked, "Will Darren know you're coming?"

"That's why I'm gonna call."

"It's kind of far. You want me to go with you?"

"No. I need to do this... man to man."

Then she asked, "Will it be a visit with the thick glass in between you two... or with you two sitting at a table with no glass?"

"Laina, why are you asking all these questions?"

She answered, "Because... you're not all that saved yet," as she took a swig of her orange juice.

Calvin chuckled a little. "Yeah, you're right. He replied while nodding. "There will be glass between us."

"Oh, good." There was a quick sigh of relief that came from Elaina. She asked, "You told Corey you're going to see him?"

"No. I may tell him afterwards."

"I must say... he's done rather well for these past few months, but... as a mom, I just wish I could do more for him. Pastor Gillesby did say if he needs counseling, he doesn't mind talking to him."

"Well... talk to Corey and see if he's up to doing that. It can't hurt."

"Yeah, maybe I will," responded Elaina as she stopped eating for a moment to mull over the thought. "I just wanna make sure we do everything in our power to help him through this, and make sure it doesn't affect his outlook on life," she explained. "They're so many kids now, who're messed up in the head because of stuff like that happening to them. Then... the craziness or depression continues as an adult."

"Yeah, I know."

Elaina said, "So, we gone nip that in the butt now."

"I agree," Calvin answered, as he stood up from the table with his empty plate and glass, and took them over to the sink. He left out of the kitchen and headed to their bedroom. Elaina was still at the table picking through bits and pieces of food left on her plate while she thought about Corey. She finally arose from the table and placed her somewhat empty plate and glass by the sink. Leaving the kitchen for Corey's bedroom, she knocked on her son's door.

"Come in."

Elaina opened his door, walked in and closed the door behind her.

"What are you up to?" she asked.

"Just finishing up some homework." He sat at his desk with a Science textbook and notebook.

Elaina sat at the foot of Corey's bed. "I just wanna talk to you really quick about something, and then you can go back to doing your homework," Elaina explained. "First of all, your dad and I are very proud of you for how you've handled things for the past several months. I know it hasn't been easy for you."

Corey nodded in agreement with what his mom was saying. "We wanna make sure we do everything we can to help you through this. Would you be against doing some counseling with Pastor Gillesby?" she asked. Corey didn't answer right away. "You don't have to answer now. Just think about it and let me know. Alright?"

"Yes, ma'am."

Elaina said, "Okay, I'll let you get back to your homework." She stood up and took a quick glance around his room. "I sure wish your brother would keep his room clean like you do. I bet he's in there right now stuffing things in his closet and under his bed to make it look like it's clean."

Corey smiled slightly and then returned to doing his homework as his mom walked out of his room, closing the door behind her. She walked to David's room, knocked one time and opened the door.

Sure enough, he was caught with clothes balled up in his arms, getting ready to throw them in the closet until his mom startled him. He looked like a deer caught in the headlights. She didn't say anything; just smiled slightly and closed his door. She continued on to her bedroom.

Elaina sat at the foot of her bed thinking to herself, "Lord, please have Corey say yes to counseling," and then, she thought about everything she needed to do for the day. Calvin had just finished brushing his teeth and coming out of their bathroom, when his cell phone rang.

"Who's calling me this early?" Calvin said to himself, but still loud enough for Elaina to hear.

"I don't know... but would like to know," she said as she looked over at him with sort of an attitude. He grabbed his cell phone off of his dresser and took a glimpse at the phone number that was showing. He answered it while Elaina's eyes were glued on him.

"T.B! What's going on, man?"

"Oh," Elaina murmured and smiled as she nodded.

"Ya boy is tying the knot!"

"What?" asked Calvin with excitement. He got Elaina's attention. "Who's the lucky lady?" Now Elaina was really paying attention as she smiled when she heard 'Who's the lucky lady?'. She already had a feeling of what Tony had said.

Tony replied, "A nice wholesome girl I've been dating for about three months named Jasmine."

"How did you meet her?"

"At a singles group gathering at my church. Man, God gave me just what I asked for and a little extra."

Calvin let out a grin and said, "I hear ya, man. Well, when is the date?"

"Next month on June 18th. You know I gotta have you as my best man."

"Yeah, of course," confirmed Calvin. "Is it gonna be in Dallas?"

"Naw, right there in Southfield. You know moms can't travel too much. So Jasmine was fine with having it there."

"Alright… well sounds like a plan, man. Just keep me posted. And I guess I need to plan a bachelor party for you… without the women," he told Tony as he felt Elaina's eyes upon him.

"Yeah, I think that's best if we wanna keep the women we have."

"Yep."

"Well, I'll hit you up soon, C.J."

"Sounds good. Later." Calvin and Tony disconnected their call.

Elaina asked, "So, Tony's getting married?" She couldn't wait until Calvin got off the phone.

"Yep! He met her at a singles group gathering at his church," replied Calvin.

"Alright now, T.B. What's her name?"

"Jasmine. And the wedding is on June 18th, right here in Southfield," Calvin explained. He added, "I knew those questions were next. So, I thought I would go ahead and appease you by answering them before you asked."

"Whatever, Calvin," responded Elaina with a smirk. "So, what do you have going on for today?"

"Getting ready to go wash these dirty cars of ours. Did you talk to Corey?"

"Yeah, I asked him. I just told him he didn't have to answer right now... to think about it and let me know."

"Okay. Well... hopefully he'll want to."

"Yeah, I'm praying he will. I wonder what's he's going to say when you tell him you went to see Darren."

"That's *if* I tell him, Laina."

Chapter 40

*E*very chair was occupied with a body either waiting for their loved one to appear or already communicating with their loved one behind the tall thick glass at the Central Michigan Correctional Facility on this particular morning in May. Calvin was among those waiting behind a thick glass booth; however, the person he was waiting for, was more so a loved one to Elaina rather than him if you asked him. It was somewhat noisy in this area with some crying and others arguing with their loved ones. Some looked as if they should possibly be on the other side of the glass.

Finally, Darren was escorted into the booth where Calvin was. He was wearing that fashionable short sleeve orange jumpsuit that the inmates couldn't resist. And also wearing a few marks on his face from someone's fist... possibly from multiple people. You could tell by his arms that he had been pumping a little iron too.

He sat down, hesitating to pick up the connecting phone at his booth while Calvin quickly pressed the one on his side to his ear. They hadn't seen each other since Darren's sentencing. Darren finally lifted up the phone.

Calvin said, "Darren."

"Hey C.J."

"I see you've already gotten acquainted with a friend or two in there," Calvin said as he stared at his face.

"Yeah... nothing I can't handle though," Darren said. "C.J., about what happened..."

"That's what I came for. I think it's time you and I talked about that. I need answers. You owe us that." Darren grabbed the front of his head and dropped his head down, shaking it from side to side. "I tell ya, Darren, you better be glad Laina had you picked up before I got back," Calvin informed him. Then, he said softly, "Because I was on my way to kill you." Darren continued to keep his head down. Calvin asked, "Just what possessed you to mess with these kids, man? And why my boy?" It was obvious that anger was beginning to rise up in Calvin, but that new inner strength inside of him began to calm him down.

He looked up and said, "C.J, I don't know. I wanted to stop... many times, but kept... finding myself—."

Calvin interrupted and said, "You took advantage of these kids. Some are gonna be scarred forever. Do you realize that?" asked Calvin. "And Corey, man..." Calvin shook his head. "He's crushed that his so called uncle would do such a thing to him." Calvin shed a tear or two, then quickly wiped his face.

Tears rolled down Darren's face. "I know. I'm sorry, man. I really am," he told him as he wiped his face. "C.J., I never told anyone this… but when I was ten, I had an uncle on my dad's side who… touched and did stuff to me," explained Darren.

The prison guard came over to Darren and tapped him on his shoulder. When Darren turned around, the prison guard held up five fingers. Darren nodded, and turned back around to Calvin.

Calvin gathered that his time was about up for visiting Darren. "So, let me get this… to fix what happened to you, you repeat what he did by doing that to other kids? There's something wrong with that, man."

"I get that, now. That's why I'm in counseling."

"Good. You need it," Calvin said, as Darren stood up. Calvin stood up, too. "I want you to know… what you did to my boy was wrong and it really hurt my family, but we still pray for you."

Darren replied, "Thanks C.J."

"Don't thank me; thank God. Because six months ago, I wouldn't've been able to say that."

Darren nodded, then hung up the phone as the prison guard tapped him on the shoulder. He turned around and the prison guard escorted him out of the visiting area. Calvin hung his phone up and left as well. They both probably had more to say, but Darren's time was up.

Chapter 41

"*W*hat's up, David?" Calvin said, as he dropped his keys off on the end table when he came through the front door after visiting Darren.

"Doing homework." David had the family room all to himself.

"Good deal. Where's everyone else?"

"Corey's in his room, Trina's in her room and momma's on the... patio, I think."

"Alright." Calvin made his way to the patio and looked through the glass sliding door where he saw his wife sitting at the table with an Essence magazine in her hands and a glass of fresh lemonade sitting on the table. It was only around 6 p.m., so, she thought she would just relax a little, while she anxiously waited for Calvin to get home. He tapped on the sliding door to get her attention. She turned around in her chair and motioned for him to come out there.

He opened the sliding door and stepped out onto the patio, closing the door behind him.

Elaina said, "Hey!"

"Hey," Calvin said, then sat down in a chair beside Elaina. He pulled her glass of lemonade to him and took a swig.

"Sure, you can have some, babe."

Calvin smiled at her and then sat her glass of lemonade back down in front of her.

She smiled and shook her head. "Well, how was the visit?"

"It went well... I guess. Somebody's been pounding on his face; I know that."

"Really?"

"Yeah." He nodded. "He really didn't have an explanation for why he messed with those boys and Corey, but he dropped a bombshell on me."

"Dropped a bombshell? What was it?" asked Elaina.

"He said when he was ten, he had an uncle who did the same stuff to him."

Her mouth dropped open.

Calvin said, "I know. I couldn't believe it either. When he told me that, I kind of felt sorry for him. Then I brought up the point that he didn't fix the problem by repeating it."

"Right!" Elaina exclaimed. "Wow." She was still stunned by that news.

"Yeah," Calvin said, as he nodded. "He actually started crying when I mentioned Corey's name."

"He did?"

Calvin replied, "Yeah, he did. And told me he's getting counseling."

"Well, that should help him hopefully."

"Yeah, I hope so," said Calvin with genuine concern. "I almost feel that I should keep visiting him."

"Maybe you should. You never know; that can help him, too. And take the Bible with you while you at it so you can share some Word with him."

"I don't know how to do that. I'm just now really learning it myself," he explained. "I'll take him a Bible, and he can read it for himself," Calvin said.

"Yeah, that'll work too. Oh… Corey said he wants to talk with Pastor!"

"Oh, yeah?"

"Yes. So, I'll take him next week or let him drive himself. I forget that he and Trina do know how to drive. I'm just not in favor of it with all the distracted drivers on the road these days."

"Well, they can drive the Benz."

"Of course they can, but not your precious Range Rover, huh?"

Calvin answered, "That's probably too big for them." He picked up Elaina's glass of lemonade and took another swig, hoping to serve as a distraction to the conversation.

"Hmm, hmm," said Elaina with a smirk on her face as she watched him drink her lemonade. "So... are you going to mention to Corey that you saw Darren in prison?"

"Umm... I'm thinking about it. I'll probably wait though, until he talks with Pastor."

"That's probably a good idea. Well... since you've about cleaned out my glass of lemonade," she picked up her glass and inspected it, "I guess we can go ahead inside and eat dinner. And then you can enjoy your *own* glass of lemonade."

Calvin chuckled a little while Elaina slightly smiled, as they both got up from the table and walked into the house.

Chapter 42

"*H*ello, young man. Can I help you?" asked the receptionist in the front lobby of High Faith International Church.

It was really quiet in the lobby; a whole different atmosphere than on Sundays and Wednesdays. It was Thursday of the following week.

"Yes ma'am. I have an appointment to see Pastor Gillesby." Corey was privileged to drive the Benz for this visit.

"What's your name?"

"Corey Hardy."

"Okay, Corey. Just sign your name in that book right there." She pointed to the three ring binder notebook sitting on the desk down on the right of her. "And I'll call and let him know you're here. Then take you to his office."

"Thank you."

"No problem," she replied. She dialed the extension for Pastor Gillesby.

"Yes, Andrea?"

"I have Corey Hardy to see you."

"Yes, you can bring him in."

"Okay, will do." She hung the phone up, then stood. "Alright, Mr. Corey... I'll take you to his office now," Andrea told him as she came from around the desk. And then escorted him down the hall to Pastor Gillesby's office. When they arrived at his door, Andrea knocked.

Pastor Gillesby said, "Yes, come on in." Andrea opened the door and let Corey in. "Hey Corey. Come on in."

Corey walked into his office.

"Have a seat."

Corey sat down in one of the two chairs in front of Pastor Gillesby's desk. "Thanks, Andrea."

"You're welcome." Andrea closed the door and returned back to her desk in the lobby.

Pastor Gillesby sat at a beautiful cherry oak wooden desk with a computer, printer, desk phone, a few pictures of his late wife and two children and a Bible on it. There were a few scattered papers on there as well, along with a couple of crosses made out of different materials, some crocheted and some ceramic. Above his head to the right were cabinets that were a part of the desk. He had a nice comfortable looking sofa in there and two book shelves filled with a plethora of different Christian books, encyclopedias, dictionaries and Bibles in every kind of translation.

He asked, "Corey, how you been?"

"Okay, I guess."

"I know these past few months or so has been tough on you. For someone your age to have to go through what you did, is not easy."

"No, it's not."

"You remember when I told you and your brother that, 'Jesus would never leave or forsake you, no matter how hard it got in your life'?"

"Yes, sir."

"Well, it's true, Corey. It was no surprise to God what happened to you."

"Then why did He allow it to happen?"

"Well Corey, the devil causes bad things to happen to people, not God. And it's usually because of the choices we humans make. In your case, it was nothing you did. So, don't blame yourself," he told Corey. "What's the man name who touched you?"

"Darren."

"It was Darren who made a bad choice. What happens is that every action we take, starts as a thought; whether it's a bad thought or good thought. Then *we* have the choice of bringing that bad or good thought into action. The mind is a playground for the devil, especially if you don't know God," he explained, as he shook his head. "And I'm gone give it to you straight, Corey. The devil hates us and he uses people to do his dirty work, if they allow it. Now, what God does is He will take a bad situation and turn it into a good one. You understand what I'm saying?"

"Yes sir, I do."

Pastor Gillesby asked, "What good so far has come out of your situation?"

"Well… it brought my dad back home early instead of staying away for three weeks."

"Okay, what else."

Corey made a slight fist and relaxed his index finger on his mouth as he contemplated. "My dad finally forgave his dad. And now my dad enjoys going to church and reading the Bible," Corey said, as he took his hand down from his mouth and looked back at Pastor Gillesby.

"You see, Corey? That's what God does because He truly does love us and wants the best for us."

"I never really thought about that. I just thought I had done something wrong that I was being punished for."

"No, not at all. Now, the devil will try to make you believe that. But that's a lie. God is going to help you get through this if you just keep your focus on Him. Alright?"

"Yes sir," replied Corey. "I appreciate you talking with me. It helped a lot."

"Anytime, Corey. Let me pray for you before you leave."

"Okay, yes sir."

They both bowed their heads.

"Lord… thank you, for bringing this young man in today. A young man you brought into this world with purpose. We pray a blessing upon him, and that your peace and anointing will rest on him as he works through the hurt caused to him. We decree and declare that he will be successful in life, be a man of valor, and be filled with your Holy Spirit. He is more than a conqueror. We thank you that no weapon formed against him shall prosper. Bless his family and show them how they can help Corey to heal also. In the mighty name of Jesus we pray, Amen."

Corey stood up and shook Pastor Gillesby's hand.

"Thank you."

"Sure thing, Corey. Call here anytime you need to talk."

"I will. See you on Sunday," Corey said. He proceeded out of the door with a smile.

Chapter 43

Corey entered in through the front door and saw his mom sitting on the sofa folding clothes when he got back. He handed her the keys to her Benz.

"Thanks for bringing my car back in one piece."

"Thanks for trusting me with driving it."

"Better you than Trina. Don't tell her I said that," said Elaina. "How did it go?"

"It went good. Pastor Gillesby is cool," Corey responded as he stood with his hands in his pockets. "He said I can come anytime and talk to him."

"That's good, Corey. I'm glad," she said with a smile.

Corey said, "I'm going to grab a snack and then do some reading."

"Okay. Your dad may stop by your room to see how your talk went also."

"That's fine," replied Corey before leaving out of the living room and heading to the kitchen.

Calvin then walked into the living room. "Did I hear Corey out here?"

"Yeah, you did. He went to the kitchen to get a snack and said he was gonna do some reading. You might wanna catch him before then, if you plan on asking him how things went with Pastor and tell him about your visit. Oh, and he brought my car back in one piece." She held up her keys dangling them while smiling at Calvin.

"What? So, now I'm supposed to let him drive the Rover?"

"I'm just saying," Elaina said, as she threw her hands up.

"Well, you can keep on saying," responded Calvin with a silly smirk on his face, as he headed into the kitchen.

Elaina smiled to herself and shook her head. Corey was sitting at the kitchen table munching on potato chips he had poured out onto a paper towel and drinking some water.

"What's up, Corey?"

"Oh, hey Dad."

Calvin pulled out a chair at the table and sat down on the side of him.

"So, what'd you think about talking with Pastor Gillesby or Pastor G as David calls him?"

"It was cool," Corey replied while nodding. "He made me realize how God's been turning my bad situation into something good. I was still thinking what happened to me was because of something I did."

As Corey talked, Calvin began eating Corey's chips. Corey was watching his every movement. Corey said, "I can't quote everything he said. I just know it all made sense."

"Well, as long as you understood what he was saying and it seemed to help, then that's all that matters."

"And Dad... don't think I don't see you eating my chips," Corey said, just as his dad was putting one in his mouth. "Get your own chips, man."

"No, I'm good."

"Yeah, because you probably had enough of mine to satisfy you," he told his dad with a smile.

Calvin just kind of snickered underneath his breath. "I came in here to talk to you and find out how things went with Pastor Gillesby, but also tell you about my visit."

"Your visit?"

"Yeah. I went and saw Darren a few days ago at the prison."

"You did? What for?"

"Because I needed answers for myself."

"Oh... okay, Corey replied.

"I wanted to know why he did those things to you and those other boys."

"What did he say?"

"He couldn't give me an answer. He did tell me though... the same thing happened to him when he was ten."

"It did?"

"That's what he said. Doesn't make an excuse for him to do that to other boys."

"No, it doesn't," replied Corey, as he dropped his eyes off of his dad and on to the table, remembering that vivid day Darren touched him.

"I believe if he would've told someone about it back then, who knows... he probably wouldn't be in the situation he's in now."

Corey looked back up at his dad. "Well Dad, I wasn't going to say anything either, to you or mom. I really didn't want to say anything to David, but I figured he wouldn't say anything," Corey explained. "Guess I should've reevaluated that."

"No. I'm glad you said something to somebody. And I'm glad David had sense enough to let your mom know," Calvin stated. "Darren has to pay for what he did, but now he's also getting some much needed counseling."

Corey said, "Well, that's good."

Calvin picked up a chip off of Corey's napkin and put it in his mouth.

After watching him, Corey said, "Dad... get your own."

"Well, you had stopped eating them," Calvin said, as he chewed

"That's because we were talking." Corey shook his head and began eating his chips quickly before his dad snagged any more.

Calvin stood up from the table and walked over to the cabinet to grab a glass. He went over to the refrigerator and opened it looking inside.

"I decided I'm gonna visit him again and take him a Bible." Corey was without words; however, displayed a look of bewilderment. Calvin pulled out the pitcher of fresh lemonade and poured some in his glass. Then, he grabbed a few ice cubes out of the freezer and dropped them into his lemonade.

"*You're* taking him a Bible?"

"That's what I said," confirmed Calvin, as he sat back down at the table with his glass of lemonade.

"Wow." Corey was still in shock, knowing that his dad hardly ever looked at a Bible, let alone, picked one up. "I'm impressed, Dad," Corey said, as he nodded.

"Whatever, man." Calvin smiled slightly at his son.

"I am. I'm proud of you, Dad."

"I'm proud of you too. You've handled things quite well, considering," said Calvin.

"I'm trying," replied Corey. "So Dad, mom said T.B. is getting married?"

"Yes, he is. Right here in Southfield. As a matter fact, I'm throwing him a bachelor party next weekend. You and David can come… I guess."

"You all having strippers there?" Corey asked excitedly.

His dad kind of chuckled as he took a sip of his lemonade.

"Naw… no strippers, Corey. If he had gotten married in our earlier years before he became saved… then most certainly." Corey laughed.

"But we'll just play some games, shoot some pool, eat and maybe have a few wine coolers."

Corey smiled and nodded.

Calvin said, "And punch or soda for David and Corey." Corey's smile quickly disappeared and traded places with his dad. He had his mind on tasting his first wine cooler, but his dad ruined that idea.

Chapter 44

*A*t the Central Michigan Correctional Facility, Calvin waited behind a few people for his turn to be checked by the prison guards. A few weeks had passed since he last visited Darren, and Calvin thought it was time for another visit. He was dressed in gym pants and an active wear short sleeve shirt, carrying a Bible in his hand. When he made it up to the prison guards, he handed one of them his Bible. The other one monitored Calvin as he placed his keys, wallet and cell phone in the bin on the belt while he entered through the metal detector. The prison guard with the Bible, thoroughly combed through it... cover to cover to make sure there were no weapons in it. Calvin waited patiently for his Bible on the other side of the metal detector after grabbing all of his articles out of the bin. The guard finally handed over the Bible to him and he continued to proceed into the visiting area.

241

This time, it was an open visiting area with planted metal tables and benches. There were a few inmates already in there visiting their loved ones.

Calvin sat down at a table in the middle of the room and placed the Bible on the table. He began looking around to see what the crowd looked like and to make sure he knew exactly where the exits were in case of an emergency. Moments later, Darren walked out from a door, searching for Calvin. He was dressed in his orange getup and the marks he wore on his face the last time Calvin saw him, were healing. There didn't appear to be any new ones; that could be seen anyway.

"Hey C.J., I wasn't expecting another visit from you," Darren said as he sat down across from Calvin.

"Yeah. I wasn't expecting another visit from me either, but it wasn't up to me. And this time I figured it would be okay not to have a glass wall in between us."

Darren chuckled a bit and said, "Laina told you to come?"

"No. I think the good man upstairs wanted me to do this… definitely not something I would do on my own," Calvin said. "Laina did suggest I bring this to you though." He pushed the Bible over to him.

Darren did a quick flip through, looking at it as if he was familiar with it at one time.

"Preciate it."

"Yeah, I'm trying to read more of it myself," stated Calvin. He glanced around the room again. "So, how's prison life?"

"It's prison. The food's nasty, my cell stinks, the bed is hard… no privacy whatsoever. Then you got men vying for position and rank, and men thinking they my boyfriend."

"Well… you should know how that feels," said Calvin quickly, without a second thought. "I'm sorry, man. The old me still comes out at times. I'm still trying to work this God thang… not quite there yet."

"No, C.J. I deserved that."

"I didn't come here to tear you down though… not on this visit. That first visit… yeah, I did, because I didn't understand why you would do such a thing to my son, somebody who called you uncle. And I was angry with you. Really angry."

"You had every right to be."

"Hear me out. But when you told me what happened to you, that *kind* of put things into perspective… which makes it a little bit easier to not wanna kill you," Calvin said with the most devilish smile on his face.

Darren's eyes stretched open. He wasn't sure if he should take that as a good thing or be really concerned for his life.

Calvin said, "My visits from now on are so you can have somebody from the outside to talk to every now and then. And I mean, *only* every now and then. This place is not just a hop and a skip from Southfield."

"Yeah, I know."

"Laina may write you... when she's ready. She's still trying to work through everything that's happened. Besides Corey, I think it hurt her the most, too."

Darren dropped his head. Calvin said, "Even though she's a spiritual woman, it's been hard on her." Calvin's attention was suddenly focused on a prison guard who walked over to a table to put a halt to some over excessive touching between an inmate and his girl. Darren lifted his head up to see what was going on when he didn't hear any talking coming from Calvin. He noticed what had Calvin's attention.

"That's wild," Calvin said, as he shook his head while turning back around to Darren.

"Man, that ain't nothing compared to some of the other stuff I've seen people try."

Calvin said, "I'm not gone even ask," as he placed his hand on his forehead, shaking his head. "Well... it's 'bout time for me to make that track back home. I've had enough of prison life today... no disrespect."

Both Calvin and Darren stood up from the table.

"None taken. I appreciate you coming, man. I really do."

"Yeah, I can't promise you *when* I'll be back. Just know I'll be back... sooner rather than later."

Darren chuckled a little.

"Alright. Tell Laina I'm really sorry for everything and thanks for the Bible."

Calvin nodded and shook Darren's hand before he began walking off.

"Hey Darren." Darren stopped and turned around. "You make sure you read it. And stay out of trouble."

Darren nodded and continued toward the exit door. Calvin watched Darren as he walked away, still with a hint of disbelief that he was really in prison.

Chapter 45

*I*t was a Saturday evening at the beginning of June when Calvin said to his son, "Corey, hand me one of those thumbtacks sitting on the table." He stood by a wall holding up one end of a sign that read 'Congratulations'. The other end was already tacked into the wall. When Corey brought him the thumbtack, he pushed it into the wall at the top corner of the sign. Calvin asked, "Is it straight, Corey?"

Corey stood back to view it. He said, "Yes." But still felt the need to survey it. "Well… straight enough, Dad."

Calvin stepped back from the sign and took a look at it for himself. He knew his son was a perfectionist, and his straight would probably be different than his.

"Yeah, that's fine," Calvin stated, then glanced over at David chilling in a nice plush chair. "David, make yourself useful and bring in that bag that has the plates and other stuff in it."

"Yes, sir."

Calvin had rented out an elaborate looking clubhouse near his home. It had nice tables and chairs, a fireplace, bar, kitchen, large screen T.V., a pool table and a foosball table. On a long table that sat by a wall, was a chicken wing platter, a large bowl of chips and a Cuban sandwich tray. And to kick in a little healthiness, he'd included a veggie tray and dip. For dessert was a chocolate cake with vanilla butter crème icing that had on it 'Congratulations Tony! Here's Your Stripper!' with a beautiful African-American woman in tasteful lingerie on it was hid away in the kitchen. On the floor were two small coolers: one with the wine coolers inside and the other with water bottles and sodas.

The place was lightly decorated with only the one Congratulations sign that Calvin hung up. He was expecting about five guys with Tony being one of them. These were guys he and Tony knew from their college days. And bless Corey and David's heart. Little did they know, they had just been invited to help their dad with setting up for the party and to aid in making the crowd look bigger.

David set up the plates, cups, napkins and plastic forks by the food, while Corey turned on the big screen T.V. Moments later, two guys came through the door. It was about 6:40 p.m. Calvin was placing a couple of chairs in a way where everyone would be together, when he noticed his friends come through the door. He headed over to them.

"What's up, Brent?" Calvin gave one of those fancy hand daps and a manly embrace.

His friend answered, "You, C.J." Brent was a somewhat tall, attractive African-American man trapped in a Caucasian body. He was in his early forties. After greeting Brent, Calvin walked over to his other friend.

"Mike!" Calvin once again gave one of those fancy hand daps and embraced him.

"C.J., what's up? So, T.B.'s gettin' hitched?" asked Mike, a handsome averaged height African-American man in his early forties also.

"Yeah, man."

"That's good. I'm happy for him," said Brent.

Another one of Calvin's buddies showed up. Calvin turned around when he heard the door open.

The man walking in shouted, "Bo in the house!" Bo walked over to where Calvin, Brent and Mike were standing.

David and Corey's attention was pretty much on the T.V. until each time the door opened. They didn't really know any of these guys except for Tony.

"C.J.!" Bo called out as he greeted Calvin. Bo's real name was Robert. Bo was an African-American man in his late thirties. He was a little on the short side, but not bad looking. Bo said, "Been a long time."

"A very long time. What… about ten years or so?" Calvin asked.

Mike and Brent were married, but not Bo.

"Yeah, I think you're right," answered Bo.

They were all huddled in somewhat of a circle.

Brent said, "It's actually been a very long time since we've gotten together like this."

"Yeah, it's been a while. You didn't happen to see Philip out there somewhere, did you?" Calvin asked.

Bo said, "No."

"We can always count on him to be late," Calvin said and then laughed as everyone else did. "Well, T.B. should be coming in soon. You guys can get something to eat. We got the T.V. going and a couple of video games. So, have at it!"

Before everyone walked off, Bo asked, "What time are the girls coming?"

Everyone wasn't saved in there, and again, not all were married. Although the T.V. had Corey and David's attention, the question reached their ears and they looked at each other and smiled at the question.

Calvin chuckled a little. "I'm afraid no girls at this party. Tony didn't want that and... I didn't either."

"What? You didn't want any?" replied Bo.

"I'm a changed man, Bo. Trying to do right by my wife and be a good example for my kids, man."

The other guys nodded.

"Hey, speaking of my kids, let me introduce you guys to my boys." He turned toward the direction of the T.V. and

249

shouted, "David, Corey!" and motioned for them to come over.

Corey and David both strayed away from the T.V. and walked over to where their dad was standing. "This is David; my aspiring pro football player." As Calvin said that, David stood up straighter and pushed out his chest a little more.

Then in a deeper voice than usual, he said, "What's up, guys?"

Calvin just smiled at his son and shook his head. Then, he said, "And this is Corey, my aspiring Cardiologist."

"Hello," Corey said, just as Tony came in the door.

Everyone's focus shifted in Tony's direction.

Calvin shouted, "The man of the hour is here!"

"Hey everybody!" Tony shouted, as the guys rushed to meet him. Calvin allowed everyone to greet Tony first before he approached him. After everyone had greeted and congratulated him, he walked up to him. He hadn't seen him in person since the altercation in Dallas.

"What's up, man?" Calvin said as he and Tony embraced. "It sure is nice not to be greeted with a fist this time."

Tony laughed and said, "Whatever, man. Good to see you." He looked around. "C.J. man, this is nice."

"All for you, my man… all for you. Well, let's get some food and see what these other guys been up to. I'm still waiting for Philip to show. You know how that is."

"Yeah. He'll get here when it's time to go home."

Calvin and Tony chuckled a bit while they walked over to the food table. The other guys were already eating. David and Corey also had a plate of food as they sat in the two big chairs in front of the T.V. Calvin and Tony took their plates and joined the other guys. About fifteen minutes later, Philip finally showed up. When he walked through the door, Calvin and his friends yelled, "C.T.P.!"

"Yeah, yeah, yeah. What's up everybody?" Philip said, as he headed to their tables; however, he stopped to speak to David and Corey first. "You guys must be C.J.'s sons."

"Yes, we are," answered Corey.

"Well, I'm Philip. You guys look like your dad."

"That's what we've been told, but I just think my brother looks like him," Corey stated. He added, "I'm Corey. He's David."

"Nice to meet you guys."

"What does C.T.P. mean?" asked David.

Philip laughed, then said, "California Time Phil."

David replied with, "Oh."

Neither him or Corey really knew what it meant; only their dad and his friends did. Philip was a somewhat tall, attractive looking African-American man in his late thirties, and single. Calvin and his buddies gave him that name in their college days.

Philip walked over to where everyone else was sitting and began bonding with them. Brent and Bo were done eating and were getting ready to play a game of pool. Mike, Tony and Calvin were still getting their grub on. After speaking and talking for a bit, Philip fetched a plate of food and joined those who were still eating.

After David and Corey cleaned their plates, they placed them in the trash. Corey grabbed something to drink and headed into the kitchen where the cake was hiding. David followed suit. Corey and his brother searched the drawers for a bottle opener. Once he found one, he used it to open his wine cooler. It was a peach fuzzy navel flavor. He took a large gulp of it.

"Not bad," Corey said, as he looked at the bottle.

As Calvin proceeded to come into the kitchen to get the cake, he stopped at the doorway when he saw his sons; however, he kept silent. Corey and David were standing by the sink with their backs toward the entrance of the kitchen.

"Let me taste it, Corey." He handed the bottle to David. Then David turned the bottle up taking a big gulp.

"How does it taste, boys?"

Both Corey and David jumped, as they turned around. David's cheeks were puffed out on each side as he held the wine in his mouth.

Corey answered, "Not bad."

David just shrugged since his mouth was full of liquid.

"Now that you two have gotten your taste out of the way, I'll take that…" Calvin grabbed the bottle out of David's hands. He still had not swallowed what he had in his mouth yet. He was still startled. "And you can go grab a soda or water."

"Yes, sir," said Corey.

David swallowed that gulp of wine cooler that was lingering in his mouth. Then stumbled out the words, "Yes, sir."

Corey and David quickly left out of the kitchen. Calvin grabbed the cake from the counter while chuckling at his sons, and then walked out of the kitchen.

"Okay, everybody… gather around," Calvin shouted, as he walked over to the food table and placed the cake there. He took the plastic cutter off from on top of the box that was supplied to cut the cake with, and stood in front of the cake so Tony and the other guys couldn't see it. "Now T.B., I didn't get you any strippers. I know you didn't want that and Laina would have my throat if I did. So… I just put one on your cake," explained Calvin, as he moved to the side so everyone could see it.

A huge grin spread across Tony's face and the others smiled and nodded. The woman on the cake was dressed in an unrevealing red corset. Tony took his cell phone out of his pocket and snapped a picture of it. Then sent it to his fiancée to assure her that he didn't have any strippers at his party.

"So I take it, you like it?"

"I love it, man."

"Good. Well, congrats again. And I'm glad you found someone who number one, loves God like you do and number two, who's not interested in married men," Calvin said, as he and Tony laughed.

Corey and David snickered. The other guys just kind of looked at each other and shrugged, wondering where that came from. Calvin and Tony took notice of their faces.

Calvin told them, "Long story, guys. We'll tell you about it one day."

After a few hours of male bonding, everyone departed the clubhouse except Calvin, Tony, Corey and David. Corey and David began cleaning up, and Tony was getting ready to head home.

"C.J., thanks for everything, man. I had a good time," Tony said, and gave him dap.

"That's what best men do, right? You on the clock now, man."

"Yeah, I know... next Saturday. I'm ready, though," Tony asserted. "Do you know how long we've been living the abstinent life? It's not easy!"

Calvin couldn't help but laugh.

Then said, "I hear ya, brother. Don't know how you lasted for this long."

Tony answered, "Definitely with God's help... for sure."

Chapter 46

*A*lthough the guys were tired from last night's party, they arose from their beds when the aroma of pancakes, syrup and sausage hit their noses. David and Corey quickly got out of bed and washed up. It was about 9:30 a.m. on Saturday.

At the kitchen table already eating pancakes with syrup, scrambled eggs and sausage patties were Elaina, Calvin and Katrina. David and Corey strolled in still half asleep, but wanted to make sure they didn't miss out on eating pancakes.

"You guys could've stayed in bed. We would've saved you some pancakes and sausage," Elaina told her sons.

"Momma, don't make promises you can't keep," Katrina said, right before she plowed her fork into another pancake from the stack sitting on a plate in the middle of the table. The boys were too tired to comment and fuss with Katrina. They just walked over to the cabinet, grabbed a plate and fork out of the drawer, took a seat at the table, then began grabbing pancakes and sausage.

Calvin was a little beat also, but needed to get on up, eat, and then run some errands to prepare for Tony's wedding.

Elaina said, "Well, Trina and I was knocked out when you guys came home. How was it?"

"It turned out really good. All the guys showed up," Calvin said.

Elaina responded, "That's good." Then there was a moment of silence.

"No, we didn't have strippers," said Calvin.

Elaina said, "What? I didn't say anything… not yet anyway."

"I knew the question was coming, though."

"You guys enjoyed yourselves?" Elaina asked, as she looked at Corey and David.

Corey answered, "Yes ma'am."

David said, "Yes ma'am, it was cool."

"Yeah, I think they had a good time hanging out with the fellas. They even," Corey and David made eye contact with their dad, and then dropped their heads to their plates, "helped me set up everything and then cleaned up afterwards."

"Oh, good," responded Elaina.

Corey and David just knew their dad was getting ready to tell their mom about the wine cooler. But Calvin had no intentions on snitching. Whatever happened at the bachelor party, stayed at the bachelor party.

Katrina didn't say anything, but she sensed there was something that wasn't told. She thought to herself, "I'll get it out of them."

Elaina asked Calvin, "You have to get fitted for your tux today, right?"

"Yeah, I do. That's the only reason why I'm up so early. Then I need to go check on the venue. You wanna go with me?"

"Yeah, I'll go."

"Good, because I can use that bulldog mentality to make sure things get done right for T.B.'s wedding." That grabbed a laugh out of the kids.

Elaina sucked her teeth and said, "Whatever, Calvin." After a moment, she asked, "Did T.B. show you a picture of his fiancée?"

"Yeah, she's pretty."

Elaina said, "I just hope he's really ready."

"Trust me… he's ready," responded Calvin, as he thought about what Tony told him as he was leaving the clubhouse.

"Well, I'm excited for him. And glad he didn't continue to pursue that homewrecker."

Calvin quickly got up from the table with his plate. He put the scraps left on his plate in the trash and placed his plate in the sink.

"Momma, you talking about Patrice?" Katrina asked.

Elaina answered, "Yes, her."

"Laina, are you gone be ready to go in thirty minutes?" Calvin asked. Somehow he knew this conversation was headed in the wrong direction and he didn't want to wake up the past.

"Mmm…," she said, as she sipped on her coffee. She looked at her watch after she put her coffee down. "Yes, I'm coming." She took a couple of more bites of her pancakes, got up from the table, and placed her plate in the sink. Then, she followed Calvin out of the kitchen. She said while walking out, "You guys know the drill…"

Katrina said, "Homework and chores."

"Yep. Make sure it all get done," Elaina said while heading out of the kitchen.

Katrina stood up from the table and walked over to the doorway of the kitchen, looking to the right to make sure her mom had gone to her bedroom. Then, she sat back down at the table. She said, "Alright, what *really* happened at the party?"

"Nothing for you to be concerned about," said Corey.

"I know what didn't happen," David said.

"What?" Katrina asked.

David answered, "Trina didn't get invited."

Corey snickered.

"You are such a butt, David! Just tell me… did they have strippers there?"

"Listen… you might as well stop prying. We're not telling you anything," said Corey.

At that moment, Katrina pushed her plate away and stood up from the table. She left the kitchen without a word.

Corey and David looked at each other, then laughed. They continued eating their breakfast. Moments later, Katrina came back carrying a large bag of Skittles. She placed them on the table and pushed them in front of Corey and David.

The boys looked at each other and then at their sister.

Corey said, "Trina… this is what I'll tell you… bribery will get you nowhere."

David laughed slightly. "It depends on the bribe, Corey. You got any money, Trina?"

"Not for you two," Katrina said, with an attitude. She had nothing else to say to her brothers. She picked her plate up and took it over to the sink to rinse it off, making it a little bit easier for her when it was time for her to wash dishes. That was one of her chores for Saturday. She came back to the table, picked up her candy and politely walked out of the kitchen.

Corey and David were just tickled about it because they loved pushing their sister's buttons.

In the bedroom, Elaina was fully dressed in casual attire as well as Calvin. They both had on jeans and a nice casual short sleeve shirt, ready for their outing. Elaina stood in the mirror of her dresser applying a little touch of color to her face and lips, while Calvin brushed his teeth in the bathroom.

"Did I tell you I have a lunch date next week?" asked Elaina.

Calvin peeked his head out of the bathroom with a mouthful of toothpaste suds and said, "Oh, wu trying to be fuddy, Laina?"

"What?" Elaina didn't understand what he had said.

Calvin spit out the toothpaste suds in his mouth and rinsed his mouth out. Then came out of the bathroom and repeated himself.

"I said, 'Oh, you trying to be funny."

"No. I really do have a lunch date."

Calvin replied, "With who?"

"Why you wanna know? You're worried?"

"No, not the least bit... but I still need to know," Calvin said, as he sprayed himself with a little cologne from off of his dresser. He turned around to Elaina.

"It's somebody who's strong, tough, assertive..." Elaina stopped applying the makeup and smiled to herself as she reflected on the person she was talking about.

Calvin glanced at her facial expression in the mirror and became silently irked. She continued saying, "Don't take no mess from anyone, has special connections and..." Elaina turned around to Calvin and said, "loves me."

"Who's the man, Laina?" Calvin asked. He was obviously disturbed at this point.

"The wo-man is my spiritual mother, Mother Newsome," responded Elaina, with a smirk.

Calvin slowly smiled. "Okay, you got me."

Elaina chuckled at him and then turned back around to the mirror to check her hair one last time.

"I'm ready. Let's go," Elaina said.

Calvin smiled to himself and shook his head. Elaina grabbed her purse from the bed and headed out of the bedroom. Calvin followed behind her.

Chapter 47

"**M**other Newsome, how do you like your smothered pork chop and gravy?" Elaina asked. She had fried chicken and fries.

"It's delicious. I didn't expect it to be better than mine... but it's close." Elaina chuckled.

"What do you eat with yours?"

"A little mashed potatoes and corn," said Mother Newsome. She had a side of cabbage and mac and cheese with her smothered pork chop and gravy for this meal. The restaurant Elaina brought her to for lunch, was a mom and pop southern food type restaurant. Elaina and her family ate there sometimes, her parents also. She knew Mother Newsome would like it.

Mother Newsome said, "I sure thank you for the invitation. I'm very selective with my invitations."

"Oh no problem, Mother Newsome. And I'm sure you are... I don't blame you," said Elaina. "It's been something I had been desiring to do for a long time. And this gives me a chance to share how things are going with my family."

"Oh, I know it's going quite well. It's written all over your face." Elaina smiled and nodded. "Well... why don't you tell me about it."

"Don't mind if I do." Elaina took a break from eating her food as she was so eager to divulge the good news about her family. "God has really showed up and showed out in my family... thanks to your prayers, Mother Newsome."

"And yours too, Elaina. God heard our prayers and honored them."

"He did. My husband has made a complete 180. Besides forgiving his dad, this man has been visiting the man that touched his son in the wrong way... *without* killing him, Mother Newsome; something the old Calvin would've done," explained Elaina.

Mother Newsome nodded and replied, "That's definitely God," while she continued to chow down on her food and watch a young African-American woman in her mid-twenties order her food at the counter.

Elaina's back was facing the young woman; however, she could tell that something had Mother Newsome's attention. The young woman had on a pair of denim low waist high cut shorts, revealing a portion of her bottom and a really low cut top.

"Would you look at that?" asked Mother Newsome.

Elaina turned around to see what she was talking about. She said, "I just don't know about some of these women. They just don't leave any of their private goods covered up these days."

Elaina quickly turned back around while Mother Newsome continued looking at the woman, and took a quick look down at her chest to make sure she was covered. She was good to go. She had on an open neck top that circled just below her shoulders along with a cardigan and a pair of dressy slacks on. Elaina replied, "No ma'am, they sure don't."

Mother Newsome finally ceased staring the young woman down and focused her attention back on Elaina. She said, "I'm sorry, baby. It's just that when I see women dressed like that, showing everything… it disturbs me."

"I agree," Elaina replied while nodding. "That's why I'm careful how I dress in front of Trina. And make sure she dresses modestly, too."

"That's right. *That's* right! Now, tell me more about your husband," Mother Newsome said. "You say he's a *new* man, huh?"

"Yes, ma'am. He's reading the Bible more, spending time with *his* dad… doing everything he can to help Corey get past what happened to him."

"How's that young man doing?"

"He has his days… but doing much better since he's been talking to Pastor."

"That's good," replied Mother Newsome. "And don't you worry about him. God's got him. He's gone be just fine," she said sternly. "And your other kids doing good?"

"Yes, ma'am, they are. David is…well… just David. And Trina is getting ready for college."

"Well isn't that something?" Mother Newsome said, as she scooped up the last little bit of her corn and put it in her mouth. Everything else was eaten up. There was just a trace of gravy and cheese left on her plate. She said, "They sure grow up fast."

"Too fast, if you ask me," Elaina said while looking at Mother Newsome's plate. Elaina was just about done with eating her fried chicken and fries. "You want some dessert, Mother Newsome?"

"Yeah, I think my stomach can stand some dessert. What'd they have that's good?"

"Umm… banana pudding and ice cream, bread pudding…"

"Say no more. I'll take the bread pudding."

Elaina chuckled, then motioned for their waitress to come to the table. An African-American woman in her late twenties came over.

"Stacey, she would like to get dessert."

"What can I get for you?"

"She would like the bread pudding and ice cream."

"I'll have it right out."

"Thank you," Elaina told the waitress.

Mother Newsome asked with a slight smile, "I get ice cream with it?"

"Yes, it comes with ice cream."

"My Lord... you gone have to roll me into my house."

Elaina chuckled as she ate the last potato off of her plate.

Mother Newsome asked, "You getting dessert, too? Because I don't share bread pudding."

Elaina chuckled again at Mother Newsome. "I guess I could though, since you paying for it."

"No, I'm fine, Mother Newsome. Help yourself and enjoy it," said Elaina. "And if I have to roll you into your house, then so be it."

Mother Newsome chuckled while Elaina smiled.

267

Chapter 48

*I*n the kitchen, Elaina was busy preparing dinner. She had a large pot of noodles boiling on the stove and a large pot of spaghetti sauce with meatballs in it. There was garlic bread baking in the oven. The house smelled like an Italian restaurant. She thought she would cook something easy since she was a little tired and still somewhat stuffed from lunch. Everyone was home except for Calvin, who would be making his way in soon. The kids were in their usual places during the evening time: David in the family room playing a video game, Trina in her room on her cell phone gabbing away, and Corey was sitting at his desk reading the Bible in his room. He'd read a little bit before he'd later come out and play the video game with his brother. Katrina wouldn't bother to come out of her room until she was called for dinner.

Calvin arrived home and he seemed to be in an exceptional good mood.

"What's up, David?"

"Hey Daddy."

Calvin watched David play for a moment. "I see you doing what you do best. Do you ever play anything else other than Madden?" he asked.

"Yes, I do."

"You see yourself on that game, don't you?

David replied, "I sure do."

"Good. Keep seeing yourself, son," Calvin told him. He focused his attention on the aroma wafting into the living room. "Boy, it smells good in here." He headed straight for the kitchen. "Hey Laina." She was at the stove stirring the sauce.

"Oh hey, babe."

"How was your lunch date?" asked Calvin.

"It was really good. I think Mother Newsome enjoyed herself… and the food. I took her to our 'lil soul food restaurant."

"Oh yeah, I'm sure she liked it. She didn't go around telling people about their lives, did she?"

Elaina chuckled and said, "No. But she did complain about how a woman was dressed."

"That doesn't surprise me."

"Well, what she was saying was true though. This girl had just about all her goodies out."

Calvin said, "Wow. I'm surprised she didn't go up to her and say something."

"Yeah, I know," Elaina answered, as she sat down at the kitchen table. "Doesn't mean she didn't want to. I think she was just enjoying her food too much."

Calvin chuckled a little. "I have to tell you something," he said, as he sat down with her.

Elaina asked, "What? Is it bad?"

"No, not at all. A co-worker of mine asked *me* to pray for him."

"Really?" asked Elaina while smiling from ear to ear.

"Yeah. When he came to my office asking me that, I had to look behind me to make sure he wasn't talking to somebody else. And then I still had to ask, 'You want *me* to pray for you?' He said, 'Yeah, I do.' He's a white guy who's an architectural draftsman. He's the one that used to live in Dallas."

"Well, where did you pray for him?"

"Right there in my office. I shut the blinds and closed the door. And said to myself, 'Okay, God... you gone give me what to say, right?' and He did just that."

"Wow... I'm speechless," replied Elaina. "He just wanted you to pray for him or was it for something specific?"

"He just found out he has cancer."

"Oh, no."

"Yeah, I know. He's a really good guy. I didn't tell him I was a Christian. So, I don't know why he asked me."

"You don't have to tell people you're Christian. Some people can just sense it," Elaina explained. "I bet you had no idea God would use you like this."

"Nope."

"Well, just know this is only the beginning, babe. God has a lot more for you to do," Elaina said. "Wait until I tell Mother Newsome!"

"Do you tell her everything, Laina?"

Elaina answered, "No... not everything. A lot of things get told to her first by God." She got up from the table and walked over to the cabinet to take plates out. "Look at God! My husband reconciled with his dad... something he said he would never do, helping his son get through his ordeal, doing prison ministry..." Calvin turned his head sideways at her with a crazy look on his face, "and now praying for people. You know what's next, right?"

"No, what?"

"You gone be preaching next."

"Naw... I'll leave that to Pastor Gillesby. I don't wanna be no preacher," responded Calvin, as he stood up from the table. He walked over to the sink to wash his hands.

Elaina hadn't said it was time to eat yet, but Calvin got the hint when she pulled the plates out. The spaghetti was done and the garlic bread was on the counter. Calvin sat back down at the table and said, "I'm just trying to be Calvin right now... a great husband to you and a great father to my kids."

"And that makes Elaina happy," said Elaina, before she shouted, "Guys, come eat!"

David, Corey and Katrina came into the kitchen without haste. They could smell the spaghetti and garlic bread from their rooms. They all sat down at the table along with their dad.

"What's up, Corey and Trina? I already spoke to David."

"Hey, Dad," said Corey.

Katrina said, "Hey Daddy."

Elaina placed plates in front of everyone, including in front of her seat. There was a plate for the spaghetti and one for the tossed salad Elaina had thrown together in a bowl. She always made sure her family got some kind of veggie in with their meals. She grabbed the garlic bread she had put in a basket and placed that on the table along with the parmesan cheese and salad dressings.

Katrina got up from the table to help her mom by grabbing some glasses for the iced tea Elaina had made. After placing the glasses on the table, Katrina grabbed the pitcher of iced tea off of the counter and brought it to the table. And then grabbed the bowl of salad as well, before she sat back down.

"Thanks, Trina," Elaina said to her daughter.

"You're welcome, Momma."

Elaina brought over the pasta and placed portions on everyone's plate. Then, she served everyone the meatball sauce. Everyone had eyes on their plates, ready to dig in. Elaina served herself last with just a little bit of spaghetti. She was still somewhat full, but wanted to enjoy the meal with her family. She was finally able to sit down. Calvin said grace and they began to go at it like a pack of wolves, especially the guys... grabbing garlic bread, salad and other things that was on the table.

Elaina said, "Guys, somebody asked your dad to pray for them today."

Katrina, Corey and David all stopped eating as they were in shock.

David said, "Somebody asked *you* to pray for them, Daddy? What were they thinking?"

Elaina said, "David!"

David murmured, "What?" and shrugged his shoulders.

"Laina, you can't hold water, can you?" said Calvin.

"Well, that's good news. I couldn't hold that."

"I was gonna tell them... myself, if given the chance," Calvin told Elaina with a slight smirk. "And yeah, David, I was asked to pray for someone. What's wrong with that?"

273

David replied, "I've just never really seen you pray before… other than say grace."

"Well, I think that's cool, Dad," Corey said.

"You told them you go to church or something, Daddy?" asked Katrina.

Calvin responded, "No. I don't know how he found out."

"Some people just know or can tell, Trina," Elaina intervened with. "And I have to say… your dad has made a tremendous change over these past months."

"Yeah, cause he was real stubborn at one time. Isn't that what you said, Momma?" asked Katrina.

Elaina laid wide eyes on Katrina with a straight face, thinking to herself, 'You have a big mouth.'

"Yeah… I was, Trina. That's true," responded Calvin, as he nodded in agreement. "And my stubbornness led to some other things that weren't right." Calvin looked at Corey and said, "It was you, Corey, who showed me I needed to change and be a better man… father and husband. You guys are important to me and I don't like to see any of my family hurt," Calvin stated as he looked at his wife and kids. "It's only because of God that I'm able to be who I am now and do what I'm doing. Now, I'm a long way from being perfect, and I'm still struggling with forgiving myself for what happened to you, Corey, but… one step at a time. Right, Corey?"

"Right, Dad," Corey replied, as he smiled slightly while nodding.

Elaina got up from the table and grabbed a paper towel from the counter and wiped her eyes before anyone could see her eyes welling up with tears. She returned to the table and continued eating. And this evening with the exception of a few other gatherings from the past months, would be forever remembered when Calvin poured out his heart to his family as a changed man.

Child Sexual Abuse Statistics

According to childsafeeducation.com, evidence suggests that:

- o As many as 1 in 4 girls is and one in 6 boys will be sexually abused before age 18.
- o Over 90% of sexual offenders are someone the child knows and trusts — a parent or other relative, teacher, camp counselor, babysitter, or family friend.
- o 30-40% are abused by a family member.
- o One out of every seven victims of child sexual abuse is age five or younger.
- o Only one in ten children who are abused will ever tell anyone.

If you suspect or know that a child has been abused or neglected, contact your local authorities right away. Or, for assistance, call the ChildHelp National Child Abuse Hotline (Staffed 24 hours daily by professional crisis counselors) at **1-800-4-A-CHILD**

About the Author

Nikki R. Miller, born and raised in beautiful St. Petersburg-Tampa, Florida, is the CEO of NRM Faith Based Films, LLC. She's an actress, singer and has recently tapped into screenwriting and now an author, with this being her first novel. However, above all of these titles, she's a wife and mother first. Nikki has always had aspirations of being on stage and/or on camera since a little girl. She began singing when she was five, singing in choruses, church choirs, stage plays and praise & worship teams as she does now. She began acting and modeling in the early 90's, when she attended John Casablanca Model & Talent School in Tampa,

Florida. From then on, she was signed to various agencies to hone in on her skills.

Needless to say, Nikki has extensive training in acting and singing, and thought this would be a long life career path for her. However, in 2014, she found out that God had other plans for her life. Unbeknownst to her, screenwriting had been added to her plans when God downloaded a faith-based screenplay called 'Change of Heart' (originally known as "Broken But Not Forsaken'). After slaving over the script for months and getting an understanding of what God had given her, Nikki realized exactly what He desired for her to do with her talents and gifts; to inspire, encourage and give hope to hurting families. That include addressing issues and topics that are usually kept quiet or swept under a rug. Yet families are being destroyed from them. With that being said, the 'Change of Heart' screenplay is now in development and preparing for production.

But that's not it… Unbeknownst to her again, in April of 2016, she found out that God had further plans for her which included *more* writing. God told her, "If you did the film, why not do the novel?" So, Nikki began writing and writing… and writing until she was finally done. Not long after completing this novel, she had a dream of giving birth to twin babies; one girl and one boy. After that dream, God had revealed to her that she had birthed a film and a book for

'Change of Heart'… the book you hold in your hands. She believes there are more births to come, and is grateful and honored that God has chosen her to be a surrogate for His messages, whether it be by film and/or book. While working on these projects, she relied on the Bible verse, "I can do *all this* through him who gives me strength." Phillipians 4:13 NIV. And leaned on the support of her husband, Johnny and sons, Jarvis and Jamar. She's also grateful for the prayers and support from her other family and friends.

Hope you enjoyed reading this book! And please, check out the movie too… when it's released!

CPSIA information can be obtained
at www.ICGtesting.com
Printed in the USA
LVHW090612040620
657367LV00006B/532